For Jess Byrd
    with admiration
    and affection.

        Jessie Bohler

May 15. 1958

REMEMBRANCE WAY

Remembrance Way

a novel by JESSIE REHDER

G. P. PUTNAM'S SONS   *New York*

Library of Congress Catalog
Card Number: 56-10241

The author wishes to thank the following authors and publishers for permission to quote briefly from the works listed:

Harcourt, Brace and Company, Inc., for the lines from "Marina" by T. S. Eliot, which appears in his *Collected Poems, 1909-1935*, published by Harcourt, Brace and Company, Inc.

Henry Holt and Company, Inc., for the line from "Death of the Hired Man" by Robert Frost, which appears in *Complete Poems of Robert Frost*. Copyright, 1930, 1949, by Henry Holt and Company, Inc. Copyright, 1936, 1948, by Robert Frost. Quoted by permission of the publishers.

The Viking Press, Inc., for the verses from "Kisses in the Train" by D. H. Lawrence, appearing in Volume I of his *Collected Poems*. Copyright, 1929, by Jonathan Cape and Harrison Smith, Inc. Quoted by permission of The Viking Press, Inc.

MANUFACTURED IN THE UNITED STATES OF AMERICA

To
Max and Hugh

Contents

The Sea

OVER the bridge of time toward the ship making its way out of New York Harbor the word *home* came drifting back to Abby Brandon who stood on the cabin deck watching the sea. The word held many places: Steeple Hill, New York, and before them Cape Fear. And yet it was not a place at all but a person. Home is Jim, she told herself. Or used to be. Used to be and was no more. But for all that he was still real, still part of her, so much so that the widening distance between them seemed to be no more than a mirage of the mind.

As she stared at the sunlit water, she began to see him in the living room at Steeple Hill, alone in the big chair with the house as still as the waters of the pool on the slope behind the house—the pool of the last day before this voyage, with the guests gone home from the party and his angry words jabbing at her. *You want too much, Abby, expect too much, and you'll be expecting it till the day you die.* The words stirring the leaves above him, and whipping up the demon in his eyes. But would the demon be gone now that he was separate from her at last?

The stamp of old questions was apparent in her eyes when she turned away from New York Harbor to glance at the form she had filled out.

SHIP: S. S. *Dixie Belle*   New York   Freight and Passengers
SAILING TIME: June 15, 1955
FIRST PORT OF CALL: Cape Town, Union of South Africa
PASSENGER'S NAME: Abigail Gregory Brandon
AGE: 32   HAIR: Brown   EYES: Dark brown
MARRIED: Yes
OCCUPATION: Photographer; lecturer, Steeple Hill University
PURPOSE OF VOYAGE: To photograph animals for a book series
NEAREST LIVING RELATIVE: Henry Gregory, brother
　　　　　　　　　　　　　 Gregory Nursery
　　　　　　　　　　　　　 Route #1
　　　　　　　　　　　　　 Cape Fear, N. C.
NOTIFY IN CASE OF DEATH: James Kirby Brandon, husband
　　　　　　　　　　　　　 Romance Languages Department
　　　　　　　　　　　　　 Steeple Hill University
　　　　　　　　　　　　　 Steeple Hill, N. C., U.S.A.

Abby turned, and stared at the deck below with its cargo marked for Cape Town, Port Elizabeth, Lourenço Marques, Beira. Her eyes were caught by the figure of a sailor with red hair whose arm went up in an arc to toss a broken crate overboard. She saw nails in the boards as they floated away. Gone, she thought suddenly, as the cargo of my mind must go before the journey is done. *Make your decision, Abby,* Jim had said. *This time really make it.* Afterward she would be free.

Perhaps the last day with Jim was a dream, she reflected, touching the ship's rail that was like a fence between her and the sea. Perhaps the day of deciding to make the voyage and the day of beginning it were no more than such stuff as dreams are made of. But if it was a dream it was taking her at last on her journey to the harbors of Africa. And beyond them lay Zanzibar, the island of enchantment that each one of us is always seeking and at the same time keeps somehow in his heart. *For we carry with us the wonders we seek without us: there is Africa and her prodigies in us.* Only Jim thought that it was one big lie.

"Safely out," the captain of the vessel spoke from beside her. He stared at the harbor and then at his heavy watch. "And not too late."

Abby looked into the eyes of the master of the vessel, a bullet-headed man of perhaps forty-five. As Captain Potter gripped his pipe she could feel him wondering what kind of woman would come alone on a trip like this one, realizing she had come—*I did have to come*—and then dismissing the thought of her. He checked the time on his watch against the time of day on the sky. He glanced back at her, ignoring the form she half-offered him, the laughter in his hard brown eyes not hidden, not intended to be hidden. "Nothing like New York where we're going."

He stood quiet, a big-shouldered man with the body of an athlete. He kept looking back toward a sinking Manhattan, with his hard brown eyes not like those of an ordinary person. And it seemed to Abby that being here with him was not ordinary at all.

"New York," he said. He stared at Abby and into her, she felt. "And then Cape Town." The eyes seeing too much, as usual. "There's only one other passenger this direction, you know, a South African lady on her way back to Joberg. Rosen is her name. Something of an invalid, I fancy. May be lonesome, this voyage." He stared. "How will you spend your time?"

"Studying," she replied, "about the animals and the country."

Thank God for the books brought from Steeple Hill and waiting in the cabin. Work would be a halter on her thoughts during the days and the long nights. It would hold her at the edge of the deeps into which too much remembrance could send her plunging. *Take your time,* Jim had told her in the paradox of his kindness. Again, in the living room, as he helped her pack the box with the notes for the book in it. *It's important, Abby. Take your time.* And his eyes watching her as if she might turn into a stranger before him.

She stared past the ship's rail toward a Manhattan that had already almost disappeared. Her eyes dark above the darker jacket, she bent forward watching the blue, incredible towers of that island of longing and damna-

tion until they were no longer apparent. Off there somewhere the woman with the lamp in her hand—*bring me
your homeless*—but here only the sea. The gulls were
dropping away, the land was behind, and the long voyage had at last begun.

She looked up toward the captain but he had walked
away, leaving her alone at the rail.

On the third night of the voyage the wind began to
freshen, driving dirty smoke down toward a rear deck
that was stumpy and cut-off looking in the sun. All secure down there, with the oil drums for Cape Town
fastened into place. The seamen working under the
lights turned the ship into a city or a factory.

"Down there." Smitty, the mate in the wrinkled khaki
shirt, who spoke in the same slurred accent as her own,
was whispering about the death and burial of a sailor on
the last voyage back. He was gesturing with his hands
as if to push dark shapes away. And it was strange. Or
at least it seemed strange, here with the sea everywhere,
and the sailors down there on deck under lights that
shut out the dark. The man had died one calm day in
the middle of the Atlantic of some ailment the mate
could not name or remember. "Down there." Smitty
pointed to the deck below. "That's where they buried
him from.

"They put him into the deep—something to see,"
Smitty whispered in awe. "With the form flag-draped,

weighted, and with the captain reading from the prayer book *for one star differeth from another star in glory. So also the resurrection of the body. It is sown in corruption; it is raised in incorruption* . . . After the body went into the deep the ship circled the burial place—*something to see*—three times."

As if to push away an obstacle, Abby lifted a hand to her forehead. That time I had the dream, she thought, the ship circled the towers of the city, and the ship rode over the earth down to the sea. All of us on the vessel knew we had died. Somehow my dead father was there, and coming to kiss me he wore the face of each following lover and I left him there, *not* in dream, when I went away to the camp in the hills that proved to be my first Zanzibar.

She turned toward her cabin as if for shelter from an engulfing sea.

There was one port of call before the ship encountered the North Atlantic. It was Charleston, with the *Dixie Belle* quiet at the dock's edge through the night and the voyage beginning again in the very early day. The day had gone now and in its place was a dusk, feather-soft above the sea. Deep this sea, so deep that in it time changed, with the present and the past beginning to move closer to each other in the movement of the vessel through the waves.

In her cabin Abby sat at the dressing table that had

become her desk. Outside, the land was gone for good, the flat earth that stretched from Charleston to Cape Fear. Gone also the bridge above the Cooper River, so much higher than the one at home from which her father had traced the horizon for her with his fingertip—*where are you now, Karl Gregory?*—and the river so much wider than the one in which he had fished. No longer the birds settling near the marshes, and behind the marshes the forests of home.

She looked up at her image facing her in the mirror. She glanced away from her own face to the form lying on the table, which she must, this time without fail, give to the captain. She picked up the paper and moved with it down the passageway into the ship's lounge.

The captain, his bullet head near a zebra-striped lamp, sat as if waiting for someone, but not for her. He took the form and glanced at it. "So you're a photographer?" He did not try to hide the mockery in his eyes. "Are you going to take snapshots of the natives?"

"I'm working on a series of books," she replied. "I'll keep on working until Beira, then go up to Zanzibar before rejoining the ship."

"Why do you want to go to Zanzibar?"

Could she tell him that she expected to find a certain Grave Island, a certain gazelle in a certain light, caught only once before?

"You can see Zanzibar Town in half a day." He spoke abruptly. "Anybody can. Ask Mrs. Rosen."

With the words pounding down on her, Abby began to feel that she was not on his ship at all. Perhaps Jim had been right all along. *You've always wanted too much, Abby. Damn-fool romantic, hunting and hoping for a nonexistent island of the mind. I can't live this way any more. We can't. Go find your island. Then come home and tell me or don't come home at all.* She came back to Captain Potter, whose stare made it obvious that he did not care whether she went to Zanzibar, or to Steeple Hill, or back down the passageway to the cabin that was part of his domain.

Abby lay on the red-painted boards of the sun deck, while the stack with its blue-white circles sent out bulges of smoke flecking the ship with soot. Now that the *Belle* was nearing the equator, the boards were hot to the flesh. She turned to get the sun on her face, lying back against her pillow, letting the thoughts run to nothing. But after a while they came again, pushing their way through the throb of the engine.

In Steeple Hill a warm day like this one would be good for the kind of party Jim had given on the day of that last quarrel. A party with the friends from the campus—old Dr. Balderson with his talk, always his talk, and Henry, too, up from Cape Fear to say good-by. Henry as brown and sharp as Karl Gregory himself used to be, a real farmer, liking to work, liking to joke with them all. Jim, and on the slope beside him that coed, her head ash-blond in the sun.

The green waters of the pool, and the sun making freckles on the earth as the light flickered through the leaves. The pleasant posturing of ideas, the afternoon going by, and afterward the unpleasant posturing that had come when the others had gone home leaving her and Jim alone, with the quarrel like a classic dance. Only you could not always count on your partner staying in his place.

Jim's words.

"Henry's been talking about you."

"Has he?"

"About your crack-up ten years ago, after he got home from the army."

"I want to forget it," she said.

And Jim, his eyes forcing themselves on hers, "You know, I think it started with that camp—Green Leaf Camp—New York—then bang! It all fits together, I see that now. Like a choker of pearls. Or a stranglehold. That summer at Green Leaf was the beginning——"

She threw words at him. "You always know all about it, Jim."

"But it was the beginning . . ."

"My God! What was the beginning of the way you were looking at that coed this afternoon?"

"Don't hit at me!"

We hit at each other, she told herself. But in the last year the hitting had taken up most of the time and he had always been more sure than she was of how to give a blow.

She turned to stare at Captain Potter who had come topside from his deck and was inspecting the big compass. "A sure one, this captain," Dannie the steward had said. Then he had told Abby about the way the captain brought his ship through fire during the war. A master —Jim kept saying that I wanted to be a master—or run away if I could not be one.

She turned suddenly, shielding her face from the man who stood by the compass.

Abby's quiet, almost ritual dinner with the captain and her fellow passenger Mrs. Rosen was over. The night watch was on, the bells rang softly in the almost tropic air, and the water persisted on every side. That evening Smitty—*something to see*—had come into the lounge and set the clock another hour nearer a Cape Town time where Abby knew the sea would be arctic cold and penguins would sit on the rock jetty that marked the entrance to the harbor. A Cape Town where Table Mountain would rise like a monster from the sea when the ship came at last into port. From the clock which had a habit of stopping fitfully as if on some time of its own, the mate had turned and smiled at her before he went topside to begin his watch.

Up there in the twilight, just before the dark shut down, this mate and Abby had begun to talk together. He had spoken of his wife: *She had me thrown in the hoosegow last spring after I got gassed up in Brooklyn when we came home from the Azores. I lost all my pay before getting home to the old lady. So I don't touch it. Never touch it again.* But while he talked the need on his face was as open as the sky above the deck and wheel. One after another he shot the stars, Jupiter, Saturn, Spica, that hung above the ship.

It was strange about the sky above the ship. For the first few days it had seemed no different from the one above the clay hills of the Piedmont at home. Then it had started coming down on her like the lid on a box. It came down when she didn't know it was moving, and it frightened her. In the same way her marriage had come down on her. One day when she looked at Jim he wore the face of the person she had married five years ago and known for fifteen. Then she looked at him again and his face, pressing at her, was the face of a stranger.

From the lounge portholes Abby looked out at the darkness that was the sea. *Don't think about Jim.* But outside the swish-stop-swish of the water began to press. Glancing from the table with its two-week-old magazines to the clock above the door, Abby saw that its hands had stopped and on the bridge deck, beginning his watch near the big compass, Smitty would not know or care.

Abby rose, went out, and stood apart from them all for a moment at the rail. Then from a deck chair that might have been a hiding place, Telma Rosen began to speak in a throaty voice and a slightly slurred accent.

"So, Mrs. Brandon, your husband is a professor," said the young woman.

"He teaches French and Spanish," said Abby Brandon, feeling old, and tired of puzzling alone.

"Why," Mrs. Rosen asked, "did you leave him?"

"I must finish my book by the time the voyage is over."

"Will you go back to him?"

"I'll go back."

"*But to him?*" Telma Rosen's voice was quiet. "Africa is a giant . . . and strange."

"So I'm told."

"Aren't you afraid, Mrs. Brandon? Going so far this way without a single friend?" She spoke again as Abby did not reply. "Were you afraid in New York?"

"Yes, Mrs. Rosen. I've been afraid there." She remembered the war-darkened streets of Manhattan, darker for her than for others. "A man came up to me once," she said suddenly. "There on the dark street, his hand tore at my dress."

Mrs. Rosen nodded wisely.

"His hand was on my breast," Abby went on. " 'Thief!' I called out. 'Thief!' "

Why *thief,* she wondered. But no use asking Mrs. Rosen. Even then, she thought, on that shadow street in New York, I was trying to buy back the past. I tried to buy it back with Jake, the boy I'd heard of at camp that summer.

It was wartime. Those crowded subways and afterward the rooms in cheap hotels. One of them had a zinc shower and a washbowl with a crack in it. I wanted to scrub all over but the need to get clean was small beside the need to get away . . . Jake had been there on furlough and was the right sort of man to marry. They had even fixed a day for the wedding . . .

"So you lived in New York during the war?" Mrs. Rosen asked.

"Yes, for a while," Abby said.

He's married now to a girl in Scarsdale, she thought. That night we smashed all hell to pieces. She remembered Harlem with the lights fogged and the rain on the pavement as they got out of the cab. The old Savoy, the gin, the two orchestras, the sweaty smell, the servicemen everywhere, that wartime year, even the Dutch Marines. Dancing with that mulatto, his hard body close to her, wanting him, but afraid, and more afraid when they went to another joint, Chez Qui. With Jake watching her as if she were insane. And she'd been insane but didn't know it . . .

"It was a strange, mixed-up time," her fellow passenger went on.

"It did not seem the time to know," said Abby, thinking of the British model in the sequin dress falling right splash into a table full of champagne bottles, and the blood everywhere. She'd kept on dancing, with the room full of smoke and her heart going hard. When Jake hit her and the Negro hit him, the place had blown up under her—and then everything fused together in the perfume of the gin, sweat, blood, rage.

"Then"—Mrs. Rosen hesitated, afraid to evoke for herself and the young girl those strange days—"You too were afraid?"

"Yes—terribly." Abby did not hesitate. "I wanted to get away." She remembered going through the city with the snow-flakes falling in bitter drifts, and the city had stopped being a city and had become a great tract of woods, a solitary tract. She had gone to the harbor to try to find a ship . . .

She must have spoken out loud.

"A ship?"

"Yes, to get away." As I am doing now on this ship, Abby thought.

Afterward her father had come to New York bringing an oblong box full of flowers from the farm, narcissus and jonquils, God, how lovely they were in that dirty room, an dhow bright his eyes had been.

Mrs. Rosen could not wait. "And you went home then?"

"Running back like a hurt bird. For almost two years clock time I stayed in Cape Fear not caring about my brother away at war, not even seeing what was happening inside my father through his changing eyes."

"You did not know your husband then?"

"At the camp. Before college and New York. Not really knowing him until he had come back from fighting."

Mrs. Rosen sighed. "I, too, am going home now, but I do not know what I shall find."

Abby, standing close to her side now, staring with her into the waters, spoke a final time: "I hope you will not be afraid."

"Only a day's run to the equator." The captain of the vessel approached them along the rail. "We're just opposite Los Island." He stared into the deep at all the marine life in the depths. "You will be photographing seal and penguin, Mrs. Brandon. Much marine life before we come to harbor. Mrs. Rosen must have seen it before."

He maketh him to have dominion over the fish of the sea, the fowl of the air—over all things except myself.

Time on the ship was not clock time. Morning was Venus hanging in the sky, a big shivering jewel low on the horizon, a jewel you were losing and did not want to lose. Noon was water so full of color it was as if blue-

ing had been dumped everywhere, spotting the sea into
brilliance. Evening was dark or moonlight and always
the dark again. This was the real time, but on the
bridge were the bells and in the lounge was the clock
which had stopped once again, halting on some time of
its own. On the chart in the passageway, each day looked
the same as the day before.

> S. S. *Dixie Belle*   11 D   12 h
> Course: 130′   Distance: 386
> R. T.: 23 h
> T Av. Speed: 17:11

The record seemed never to change, but each day,
each minute, was different from the one that went before and from the one that came afterward. Yet there
was a continuous resemblance and you learned to recog-
nize that, too. This day, which was the one of crossing
the equator, brought a dull morning with the tropic
sea closed into its circle of gray and with Smithers on
the bridge checking the course by compass instead of fixing the angles by the sextant.

Abby sat at the lunch table watching Dannie the
steward place an engraved scroll beside her plate because it was customary to place one there. The equator,
she thought. A line on the chart in the passageway. In
Cape Fear, when she was a child there in the time after
her mother died, she had a book about the equator and
how on the ship there was always a party to which you
were certain to be invited. The master of the vessel be-

came Neptune, and the sailors danced a hornpipe, or at least they had danced it in Abby's mind.

You get strange ideas when you are a child, she told herself, looking past Dannie who stood at the serving table, his lost sea-gull eyes fixed on the sea. The one you had about the bird: as you passed by the equator, a great white shape of an albatross had hung over the stern of the ship watching everything that went on with a benevolent eye. To have him there made you know you had come into safe waters past a line that God himself had marked down on the sea. And the bird had looked at you with the eye of God.

But there was no bird anywhere, and the line you once thought was made of tarred rope was invisible, after all. The truth was that crossing the equator was like crossing all the other latitudes. You did not know they were behind you until the boundaries were marked and you had come to a new region. You never knew the moment of the passing, even though you might see it on the face of a clock. For no one minute was by itself or was the mark of a separate place. You knew neither the time nor the place until both were behind you and could never be changed.

"Coffee?" Dannie asked. And when she shook her head. "I'll put the scroll in the cabin for you."

She thanked him, and pushed back her chair. It was like that summer of the camp when Jim went to Furlong for football and got the hurt shoulder that turned him into a scholar. It was like that again when he came to Steeple Hill after the war and they had at last been together. Abby moved back to that night from the starboard deck of the *Belle*. *Grow old along with me,* he had said, a new twist in his smile. *The worst is yet to come.*

Abby leaned against the rail, and stared at the deck below which was flecked with soot from the cut-off smokestack. Down there the ship's carpenter was building an oblong box. Like a coffin. You *do* get strange ideas on shipboard—ideas about not getting back where you came from even though your ticket says you can reverse yourself at the far point of the journey and start home again. I tried to start over again with Jim, just after graduation, before going to New York, she told herself. But it was no good.

So she had gone to the city, and got a job, and before very long had begun the drinking, the little death the soft-voiced mate was inviting now near the compass on the top deck of the *Belle*. And then that morning of waking up in a strange room, not knowing where or how. A point of no return I did not acknowledge, Abby decided, refusing to look at the shape of the box on the deck below. *You really do not need a box to get buried in.* Or she had not acknowledged it until too late.

For even in New York, she thought, shivering a little under the gray sky, when the agency job was bringing me what seemed to be a lot of money for those days, I still wanted to buy back the past. I tried to buy back

Jim's face with all the strangers' faces that came to be too well known. The good ones, the bad ones, the useless search running out over the war years. The handsome faces, the ugly ones, mixed up with the faces of the city, with images forgotten in time and not one of them was the right one, after all.

She looked again at the box on the deck below. The death, if not of the body, had come as it had had to come, in the city. *A crack-up is a stranglehold.* It had come with no psychiatrist to hold a wake for childhood —or for any other time. In a dirty Manhattan room filled with delusions and fear flapping everywhere like a great dark bird, a damnable thing, a rotten one, pushing at you, clinging to you, and always there, the great dark bird. And then the wriggling to get free had begun.

Afterward, when Jim had come back and she'd married him, it was another starting place, even though she had known for certain by then that there would never be another starting place.

Good-by to the buried life, Abby, from now on we're going to spout about it. On the island with his arms around her, and that terry-cloth shirt she still wore, she'd felt warm and safe, or as warm and safe as anyone can feel after destruction. That white beach, the water the color of emeralds—watching the native boys bringing the horses to shore to bathe them. Never saw horses have such a good time . . . being with Jim in the islands was lovely.

At first, after the marriage, almost the best thing about it was that he knew all about the camp and the trouble there—where *was* the beginning—and told her to put it away and not dig it up again. He knew about New York and pretended not to mind, and at first maybe he really did not mind, but then the trouble began. *Make up your mind, Abby. This time really make it up.*

Jim in Steeple Hill and what time was it there? Perhaps it did not matter. She did not have to decide about him yet. Not yet. That was not her world. Hers was here under a sky more gray than before, and the silence of the sea everywhere.

She looked past the box on the deck below and up at the sky. Behind the clouds were the cold spaces where her father had gone into the night. But it was no good to want him back, no good at all. She kept looking at the color-gone sky. Behind it were spaces that were closer to her now than they had been when this voyage began.

And another invisible line was left in the wake of the vessel.

By the time the *Belle* neared Ascension Island the movement of the ship was so familiar that it was as if the steadiness of land had never existed at all. The ship was different, too, alive in the topmost swirl of smoke as it plumed from the stack and in the rolling thrust of the great screw in its belly. Behind the screw the wake, and ahead the long swells through which the *Belle* moved steadily toward the Cape Town harbor and the first discharge of cargo. Africa, so far away that last day in Charleston, grew close.

Abby opened the book that lay on the table before her. *Near Zanzibar are small coral islands, the sea water colored in blue and green. Of one of these islands, Bagamoyo, terminus of an old slave route, and starting point for caravans, Richard Burton, the explorer, has written . . .* On another, Grave Island, the Zanzibar, Suni . . . But for all these enchanting words it was lonely here in her cabin. And this morning the sea of the Southern Hemisphere was definitely threatening.

From the mirror, across the desk, Abby leaned forward, putting the book on the cabin floor beside the chair. Maybe the running away, as Jim called it, had begun at Green Leaf Camp that summer of her first disgrace. She shut her eyes against the night of that disgrace in the cabin by the lake and closed her ears against the accusing whispers that had followed her about the camp. Instead of the knowing eyes and knowing faces of the other girls she tried to see the subway faces, the war-dark street faces, but saw again only her own face in that guilt-flashed moment of apprehension in the cabin by the lake.

I'm dreaming too much, she thought, going back to my youth and trying to find a reason for leaving Jim. I don't need a reason. If I cannot accept him and let him accept me, then we must find a way to get along without each other. If I am as much in need of escape as he thinks I am, then it won't be any good with him. Perhaps I do want more love from him than he can give to me. And from everyone I come close to, starting back with the camp, Abby thought, lying back in the chair from which she could see through the porthole the wild white clouds.

When nighttime came, after saying good night to Telma Rosen she lay in her berth at the line between sleep and waking, with the movement of the ship rougher than it had been until now. It was as if the *Belle* went on her way, tossing and pitching and cursing in an attempt to find the path to harbor. Abby also tossed, almost sleeping and afterward coming into wakefulness again. Where were they now? What night was this? *What seas what shores what gray rocks and what islands? What water lapping at the bow, and scent of pine and the woodthrush singing through the fog? What images return, O my daughter.* What time was it in Steeple Hill? In the name of God what time was it on the *Dixie Belle?* And what was the hour on Arcturus? Would Captain Potter, if he ever deigned to notice her, tell her the time?

And dreaming at last, she found the ship so tall that the masts were brighter than Arcturus in the sky. She had come at last to Zanzibar, with the sails on the dhows the same dun color as the tents the girls at Green Leaf had used for sleeping in the open. And everywhere near the island the water was filled with great white lilies. Picking the lilies was a girl whose figure she could see in the distance as she rode the ship down the street to Zanzibar.

Then, suddenly, the ship turned around and took her back home to Cape Fear where the yard glowed with the camellias her mother had planted near the porch the year before she died. But at the porch the ship veered, and in her dream, only it was too real for dream, the ship rolled as it sometimes did at night, only this was no rolling that she could come back from. When she dived into the deep sea, just before she went down, she felt the arms of her mother around her. She cried out to her across the engulfing years but before her mother could call back Abby awoke.

In waking she turned on the light above the berth, still trying to escape the rolling over of the ship. Later, at the table, she shuffled aimlessly through the papers that were heaped together. Even with the light on, the fear was in her, pressing forward from the darkness outside and leaving no escape. And when she began to read the policy she had bought for Jim the fear was greater than before, greater than the one that had beset her in the dream.

POLICY 1467432

For the loss of life	The principal sum
For the loss of both hands or both feet or sight of both eyes	The principal sum
For the loss of one hand and one foot	The principal sum
For the loss of either hand or foot or sight of one eye	One half of the principal sum
For the loss of thumb and index finger of either hand	One fourth of the principal sum

If the body of the insured has not been found within six months after the disappearance, stranding, sinking or wrecking of any means of transportation not hereinafter excluded, loss of life resulting from such injuries shall be presumed to have occurred . . . loss caused by exposure to the elements following a forced landing, stranding, sinking . . .

Beneficiary—she glanced to the end of the policy—*James Kirby Brandon.* But if I leave him, she thought frantically, the policy will belong to Henry. She shoved the paper into a drawer and eyed with dark distaste her own image in the mirror. It was time to stop dismembering the years of strandings and of sinkings. But how could you stop when each day took you back to another day, when each year took you back to the one that went before and before? You find yourself rolling with the ship, moving back into that spring when the world was beautiful, or seemed to be, and when you neither had a policy against death nor knew you would ever need one.

The Shore

ONE

IN THAT Cape Fear spring of long ago the whole world had been beautiful, or had seemed to be. The water oaks near the Gregory farmhouse, keeping the leaves of last year, had been chartreuse in the afternoon sun, but near the barn a swamp maple blazed red. Through the barn door, as she came toward it, Abby Gregory could see her father at the worktable thumbing through his shipping orders for Saturday morning. Dark, with his face roughened by the sun, and with a lean, spare body, he stood near the table touching his papers with fingers that were dusty from planting.

After a moment he turned away to stare past his daughter at the north field from which the jonquils would be taken for shipping in the morning as soon as the light was good. A long task, the cutting of the blossoms, and afterward more work of packing the flowers that were to be picked up by the express truck at noon. Suddenly he turned to Abby as though the necessity for the task ahead had been lost in the realization of her image beside him. But he spoke of the jonquils.

"I may take a few of them out of the field this afternoon when I'm through working," he said.

Abby glanced at the dark eyes, the mouth with the half-twist that might have been a smile. Beside him she looked small, and yet there was a quickness of movement about her that matched his own. Her face, dark like his but delicate, wore the surface assurance that sometimes masks a sea of uncertainty. When she spoke, her words came with a faint hesitance, as if her question in the moment of asking it somehow became a discovery.

"Aren't you through working yet?"

"I would be if Miss Anson Vann hadn't called me up again."

"What for this time?"

He rubbed the back of his hand against the stubble of beard that was a thick shadow on his chin.

"All she ever wants is the best I've got in the nursery."

"Did she get it?"

"I kept saying my stock was low. Didn't have any decent camellias for her." The half-twist of a smile came again. "She finally decided on those two big Pink Perfections at a price I'm ashamed of."

Abby stared at him soberly.

"You didn't really want to sell them, did you?"

For a moment he stood beside her without replying, almost as if he had not heard the query. He kept staring at the fields where long shadows from the pine forest behind the fence were beginning to dull the gold of the flowers. On his face lay a look of belonging, and of always having belonged. This was his own place, this lowland farm, and he was as much a part of it as his flowers, as the roots that went down deep into the earth from the long spikes of the pines. He turned at last to speak to her.

"I don't like to send my flowers away."

He stared again at the long table where the Negro workers, before going home for the day, had arranged a row of cardboard boxes with green wax-paper linings. Tomorrow the jonquils would lie in these nests, sticky stems bound with strings, bunches of flowers wedged under wooden staples to hold the blooms in place for the journey. *Gregory Flowers Grow the Best,* with the labels repeating themselves along the length of the table.

"We'll ship fifty dozen if the weather holds," her father told her.

"Will it hold?"

"Looks that way." He brushed her shoulder with his hand. "Since there's no school tomorrow, you'll be here to help with the packing."

"I may have to go to town in the morning," Abby said hesitantly.

"To town?"

"Yes."

He took a cigar from his pocket and began peeling away the wrapper.

"You have your basketball game tonight. Then the party tomorrow. I thought sure you'd stay in the morning to help with the jonquils."

"Miss Matthis telephoned me a little while ago from the high school," she said. "After you went in the field."

"What did she want?"

"She may want me to come into town for a talk with a friend of Miss Anson Vann."

"Talk about what?"

"This friend owns a camp in the mountains," Abby explained. "Girls go there for the summer months and Miss Anson thought I might like to go."

"Why would she think that?"

"Her niece from Charleston goes to the camp and Miss Anson wants . . ."

"Anson's always wanting something," her father said abruptly. "My camellias. My daughter."

He turned and went to the barn door and stood there staring past pines that had a darker glint than before in the fading sunlight. For a long time he kept looking past the trees at the house on the other side of the field, as if for a familiar figure. But when his sister Janie came into the yard to touch the clothes she had hung on the line to dry, to touch them and, finding them still wet, turn away, Karl did not seem to be aware of her at all.

"You were reading late again last night, Abby," he said.

"Miss Matthis lent me a book of hers."

He put his cigar into his mouth and bit down hard on the tobacco.

"I read that little writeup in the paper about your basketball game tonight."

"It's hard to believe this is the last time I'll be playing."

"Wish I could be there to watch you, but we're having a growers' meeting. Japanese beetle control. I'll take you to the high school and pick you up when I come home." He looked at Abby shrewdly. "Will Miss Matthis be at the game?"

"I don't know."

"You tell her not to go making any fancy plans for your summer. I want you at home."

The word "home" left his lips to jar past her, to embrace the fields, the shed, and the house beyond them. In Abby's mind it became a circle, holding her here and shutting her away from a larger space. What were those words in the book the teacher had given her? *Home is the place where when you have to go there they have to take you in.* But perhaps it was a place you had to leave behind you, even though they had taken you in and wanted to keep you there. Or a place from which you had to shake yourself free. And far ahead it might become a place you had left long ago, a place that had become changed in your mind even before your departure.

"Miss Matthis wants me to have a change," she said to her father.

"You don't need any change." Her father spoke abruptly. "This friend of Miss Anson Vann. You say she's coming to Cape Fear?"

"She's driving up from Charleston this afternoon."

"What's her name?"

"Mrs. Stephens."

"And where's her camp?"

"It's up near Flat Rock."

"That's clean across the state."

"Of course it is. Girls go there from a lot farther away than Cape Fear. They go from New York."

"What kind of girls?"

Abby flushed darkly.

"The best girls from everywhere."

"Like Anson Vann's niece?" he wanted to know.

"I'm sure it's a good place." Abby spoke savagely. "I'm just sure it is."

"I've been to Flat Rock, and it's nice enough," he replied. "But we got a good place right here."

With the words closing over her in spite of her desire to stay free of them, she stood staring at the maple and at the fields beyond it. The farm *was* a good place, especially in early spring, with the air carrying a fragrant smell and the clouds straying in from the beach not far away, bringing winds that often held an echo of the restlessness of the sea. But for a long time she had known that it would never be so good again as it had been before her mother's death. Not even on a spring afternoon like this one, with her father standing close to her at the edge of the field.

"I'd better start getting dressed for the game," she said. "Aren't you coming to supper?"

"I'll be there after I bag up the camellias. When I get done with them I can forget about Anson Vann until she catches up with me again."

"You don't really want to forget her," Abby said. "If you did, nobody would be left to bother you."

Her father took the cigar from his mouth, letting the words come slowly from his lips.

"Anson Vann's not so bad," he said. "At least that's what your mother used to say."

He walked away from her toward the shed where the camellias waited for the bagging. *That's what your mother used to say.* With the words time tipped backward so that Abby almost expected to see a remembered figure beside her in the field, the light hair framing the face. That visage of yesterday was so real that it almost became part of now. Time began to fuse, with all the days together like minutes in an hour, separate and yet touching. It seemed then that her mother was beside her again. Only now Abby could not find the face.

She turned, and walked away from the barn toward the farmhouse that was home.

TWO

DEREE STEPHENS drove along the highway past the Gregory farm, with the greater part of the journey home to New York behind her, the spring circuit for the camp work complete, and the prospect of a good season lying ahead. Catching sight of Turtle Fountain, she turned as Anson Vann's niece Emmy had directed her, pulled the car to a stop in front of a tall brick house with windows that had not as yet been shuttered against the heat of the low-country summer, and went up the path to the front door.

After a moment Miss Anson Vann, wearing a sweater open at the throat with a wedge of skin cream-white against the wool, appeared before her guest, speaking softly in welcome. When she beckoned Deree into the hall, the smile on her face was so like the smile on the

face of an ancestor whose portrait hung above a mantel
that it was as if she had pinned part of herself on the
wall. But the indoor light made her handsomer than the
sunshine of the porch.

"I was late getting started this morning," Deree said.
"But here I am."

"And here to stay awhile with me." The words were
a command.

"Not this time, I'm afraid."

"But why not?"

"I finished most of my camp work before leaving
Charleston———"

Anson took her friend's arm. "Tad will bring your
bags. I've put you in the downstairs room."

In her bedroom with its cherrywood chest and pale
chintz the visitor slipped out of her woolly coat as the
Negro boy brought the luggage. At the dressing table
she patted her face with powder and afterward pulled
on a pastel jacket that heightened the delicate pink
tones of her cheeks. When Anson knocked, she swung
around, standing like a Watteau figure, lost and fragile
in this park of a house, fragile and somehow sure.

"I really must go by Monday, Anson."

"No reason if you've finished your work in Charleston."

"I have my girls for the summer, but now the work
of preparing for them begins." She walked behind her
friend toward the porch.

"Emmy told me when she phoned this morning that you had many applicants."

Deree sat down and accepted a cup of tea.

"It's always good to be able to turn them away."

Across from her, Anson gave a small cough.

"I wish I'd waited until you came to speak to Miss Matthis about the camp."

"Miss Matthis?"

"One of our Cape Fear teachers has a room in the house next door. She asked me the other day about your taking one of our girls at Green Leaf—one Miss Matthis thinks may go a long way."

"Do you know the girl?"

"I buy flowers from her father."

Deree looked gravely into her cup.

"I'm afraid a man like that couldn't afford Green Leaf."

"Karl Gregory could send her if he chose."

"At any rate, it's too late. We're filled for the summer."

As a woman opened the screen door of the house across the way Deree gestured toward her.

"Is that your friend?"

"She's on her way to supper."

"We *are* filled, Anson. Perhaps you'd better call her now and tell her so."

Anson beckoned to the teacher who had started down the path that led to the street.

"Perhaps you'll tell her yourself, Deree," she half-whispered in apology.

She stood up to meet the teacher who came stiffly toward them across the young grass of the lawn. Still stiff, Miss Matthis spoke in greeting and then sat down across from a Deree Stephens who was as smooth as a brushed tabby and as mild as the cream in the pitcher.

"Anson's been talking to me about your interest in my camp." Deree leaned toward the teacher across the table.

Anson spoke in embarrassment.

"My friend's just been telling me that Green Leaf is filled for the summer."

"But this afternoon I spoke to Abby about going there."

Deree offered a china smile.

"I'd really like to help you out." And surface polite. "If you don't mind my asking, why are you so interested in this girl?"

"Abby isn't just a girl."

Anson spoke vaguely.

"She's good at playing games, I believe."

"She's my best student." The teacher's nose looked more pinched than before. "She writes well, and lately she's begun to take photographs for the yearbook."

"Her father showed me a snapshot of hers." Anson spoke nervously. "Really, quite good."

Deree began to pretend an interest.

"Would her parents want her to come to us?"

"Her father might protest, but he'll do what's best."

"And the mother?"

"She died some time ago."

"The girl's lonely—is that it?"

"An aunt lives at the farm. And a younger brother. But Abby needs to reach out from them."

"Where did you first hear about my camp?" Deree asked.

"At the university last summer. At Steeple Hill everyone says your camp is the best in the South."

"We think so."

"In fact, I've never heard anything but the very best about it."

Deree's face began to show a deeper color. She drew back a little, as if to remove herself from the teacher and have done with it. But something, it may have been hope in Miss Matthis' eyes, or perhaps it was the echo of the compliment that had come from the visitor a moment before, brought her forward with her own words not exactly those she had expected them to be.

"If this girl's all you say she is—and since Anson's interested in her, too—I might at least have a look at her. Each season we do save a few places for scholarship girls."

The teacher spoke quickly.

"Abby's playing basketball tonight. Would you be willing to come to the gymnasium? I have a meeting at eight but I can meet you there and stay with you till the game begins."

"I really don't know——" Deree wavered.

"You don't have to stay unless you're impressed by Abby." The teacher stood up. "I want her—more than you know—to go to a camp like yours. One she will always remember."

With a sudden gesture of decision, Deree also stood to stare down at the brown sparrow face of her hostess.

"Have you ever seen a basketball game, Anson?" she wanted to know.

"Of course not."

"Then it's time you saw one. We'll meet you there, Miss Matthis." As the teacher turned to go she added gracefully, "With a camp like mine you can never really tell. It just might be that this Abby Gregory is my girl."

THREE

IN THE front bedroom of the Gregory house, where her mother's pine bed stood in the corner, Abby began to dress for the game. With agile fingers she jerked her blouse over her head, roughing her dark hair, not troubling to smooth it down. She took shorts from the closet, thrusting her straight legs through the khaki with quick motions. Near the mirror she paused to look at her own image tentatively and then lost any thought of herself in the thought of the game that lay ahead.

The contest tonight, the last she would play before going to the university at Steeple Hill next year, might be close but Abby knew her team would win. They always won when her fingers were as cold as they were now and her stomach quivered under her blouse. She knew her team would win, but she did wish that the score were already on the board and the game behind her. Then she could see it as a thing accomplished, without the isolated element of doubt that always stuck in her throat like a crumb. She turned from the mirror and stood very straight.

"Aunt Janie," she called, her voice more tense than usual. "Is my sweater ready?"

Her aunt came into the room holding the garment at arm's length, as if it were a fish she had just caught.

"Aren't you ever going to let me buy you a new sweater?" she asked.

"I like this one." Her aunt did not understand that this garment with its worn and broken strands had long ago become for her the symbol of the only invincibility she had ever known. "I wish you could come to the game," she added.

"Henry and I have to stay home to do his lessons. He's

let them go again." The aunt paused at the door and turned to stare at her niece, at the hair still tousled a little, the eyes on fire with desire for the game. "I fixed the hem of your party dress," she said.

Abby sat down on the bed, losing the concentrated look of a moment before when the game, glittering like a light at the end of a corridor, had been her only thought. The dance at the country club to which Jim Brandon was taking her tomorrow night must soon be faced. Even being Jim's date could not drown her distrust of this gathering where slick-haired boys guarding girls with tea-rose faces would be predominant.

"I hope you like the dress," Janie said tentatively.

Abby stared at the closet where the garment her aunt had chosen hung among the simpler clothes. Tonight would bring the contest that for a little while, at least, could make her forget every doubt in the playing. Tomorrow the dance, the music, the country-club girls in their glittering dresses, and her own dress swirling around her as she danced with Jim. But that was tomorrow.

She looked up as her father called from the living room downstairs.

"Come on, Abby. Let's go."

In the car, as the Ford jogged along the dark road, she sat with her hands folded, wearing an air of concentration that set her apart from her father. In the night, she was like an Atalanta, cold, virginal, with no thought except victory. Silhouetted against the street lights, her profile had a relentless air of victory. After he had pulled the car to a stop, her father punched her gently.

"Here we are," he said.

She left him with a quick good-by and walked into the dusty lobby of the high school. The muscles in her stomach were tighter than before, and as she walked her feet seemed hardly to touch the floor. The objects she noticed every day—the statue of Poe's raven that was more like an owl, and the big photograph of the sand dunes at the beach she wished she had taken—did not exist for her tonight. She saw only the bright lights of the gymnasium down the hall, heard nothing but the voices of the players as they shouted to one another while they practiced.

"You'd better hurry, Abby," someone called.

She rushed past the bench, not pausing to take off her sweater. Joining the other players in practice, she was, even in the first moments, safe in her world. She caught the ball a teammate threw her, and dribbled down the black marked floor and twirled the sphere into the net over her shoulder with seeming carelessness. Absorbed in the power of her own body, she was unconscious of a superiority that was already obvious to the spectators.

"Yea . . . team . . . ray . . . team . . . rah, rah!"

She was oblivious to the cheers that sifted down from the balcony and unaware of Miss Matthis, late for her teachers' meeting but still lingering in the gymnasium. Nor did Abby see the face of the stranger who stood beside the teacher. Deree Stephens peered down at the court with a patient interest that was not reflected in the face of Miss Anson Vann who kept thinking of the way they had hurried over a crab salad.

"She's the dark, shy one," Miss Matthis said.

On the court below, tossing the ball toward the net, Abby was even more intent than she had been on the ride to the gymnasium with her father. Every move displayed a fine precision and an awareness of the precision. The free, lovely motion of running toward the basket and of waiting for the ball to drop through the net brought the peace her father must feel when he stood staring into the fields that belonged to him.

"Yea . . . team, ray . . . team!"

The referee called a "ready, play," and the game began. Abby missed one shot, feinted, backed away from a guard, and finally, with a flip of the wrist, found the basket where the ball hovered over the rim and swished into the net for the first score of the evening. As the cheers rose, she heard her own name vaguely and the long hurrahs not at all. They were like a satire on a Greek chorus, performed by people who did not belong in the play.

Near the end of the half, when the Cape Fear team was in the lead, the crowd in the balcony began to take on the tense expectancy of people watching an execution and wondering how terrible the slaughter would be. Deree Stephens stood straighter, and touched her pink-tipped fingers together in excitement. On the court below the players settled into geometric patterns and then broke into chaos again with Mrs. Stephens watching Abby instead of shifting figures.

"Half—half!"

The referee blew the whistle, looking at Abby as if he were uncertain whether she would obey the signal. She came to a perfectly timed stop and walked to the bench. The color was high in her cheeks but under it her skin was smooth as cream. A faint line of perspiration sat like dew on her upper lip but she did not bother to wipe it off. Away from the other players she sat very quiet, her only desire to hear the noise of the whistle that would start the action again. To be caught up in the hard contact the contest brought, to lose oneself in a sudden rush down the court, to leap high into the air after the ball, was like ascending to heaven.

Afterward, it would be fine, too, when her father had driven her home, to lie between cool sheets and listen to the wind moving in from the sea to the oaks outside her window. Then she would be quiet, not excited as she was when she sent a ball toward the net, or unlike herself as she would feel in the evening dress her aunt had bought her. Lying in her mother's bed, all that would matter to her would be the sweet night wind and the tired feeling that comes before the dark of sleep.

Abby moved uncomfortably on the bench, wondering suddenly whether she would ever be able to do anything well except play this game.

"The half's not starting this minute," someone said over her shoulder. "Don't wear yourself out before it begins."

She turned and saw Jim Brandon, who had come across the court and was leaning nonchalantly against the wall.

"Hello, Jim."

"Nice game you're playing. Put your sweater on or you'll go stiff."

She stood up beside him, pulling the sweater tight around her neck. The two of them leaned against the wall, their shoulders close, like figures in a frieze. Jim towered above Abby but in her own way she was as perfect as he. His blunt fingers might have twisted an iron bar, while hers, which were also strong, had a delicacy about them that would make a flower safe.

"They're on to your short shots, Abby," he said. "You'll have to try something else. Better play nearer the foul line. Even if you miss, it's better than getting nowhere."

"I'll play it from the outside."

"Well, take it easy. You want to be in shape tomorrow for the party."

As he walked away she stared after him. Jim would feel easy at the party, with the college crowd home for the weekend. To him a dance, a game, or people who might be more certain than you were nothing to worry about. The sureness was almost as apparent as the football emblem he wore on his sweater. While she, even with Jim, when they were together in the car and he kissed her, felt frightened—and the look on his face then was like an animal from the woods.

As the whistle shrilled, the news that the half was about to begin, the face faded. She stripped off her sweater, and ran out on the court, forgetful of everything in a hard excitement. While she practiced her shots the gymnasium shrunk around her until it became a world in miniature. With every practice shot she became more sure of herself. The harsh blue lights in the gallery, the singsong cheers of the crowd, the new springiness in her legs brought a superb physical delight.

"Ray . . . ray . . . Cape Fear!"

The sound of the cheering died and the second half got under way. Abby's playing fell into the most perfect pattern imaginable. Her body responded before her mind instructed it; her fingers, knowing which way the ball would go, reached for it before the sphere came in her direction. Once she had the ball in her hands and was passing it back and forth she went down the court to the best spot for a goal so fast that she shook her opponents away from her as though they were flies.

Everything about the game Abby had ever known returned to her. The long afternoons in the gymnasium, when she had stayed after the others went home and tossed the ball through the shadows until she learned to know where it was going without following it with her eyes, fused into this moment. She was not one girl but all the girls she had been from the day after her mother's death when she walked across the court with her rapid stride, picked up the ball, and threw it at the goal to watch it drop perfectly through the net.

As the half progressed she played in a rhythm of her own. She lost the sense of the forms of her fellow players around her, forgot the passage of time, and moved down the court with a classic grace that brought the spectators to their tiptoes and made the crowd in the gallery break into new cheers.

She kept clear of the goal where the guards hovered with upraised hands and moved near the circle, shooting the ball from her chest. Afraid to change their defense, the guards stood in their positions while she moved before them like a ballerina. A few of her shots went wild, rattling off the backboard into waiting hands, but more often the ball rolled around the rim and dropped into the net. She kept working back until she appeared to be in a space by herself.

The instant before the whistle blew that ended the game she tossed a long shot. The ball arched through the air like a bird, going so high that for a moment it gave the illusion of breaking through the skylight and disappearing. Before it began to fall, Abby lost interest in it. With the superb nonchalance that comes only when a person knows he has done a thing perfectly, she turned and walked away from the goal.

From the balcony, where the teacher had left them, Deree Stephens with Anson Vann beside her went silently through the side door and into a street where the wind was sharper than it had been when they left Market Way to come to the game. Neither of them spoke until after the raucous, still-cheering crowd in the gymnasium was far behind. As they drove along the avenue where the yellow eyes of the houses kept staring at them, Deree pulled her jacket close about her shoulders.

"I can tell you now, Anson," she said. "I want that girl for Green Leaf."

FOUR

ABBY walked a little uncertainly past the fountain with its sea creatures anchored in stone toward her meeting with Mrs. Stephens. At the door of Miss Anson Vann's house she touched the bell, and touched it again, telling herself that this was just a talk, and certain to be no more difficult than the one with the professor from Steeple Hill about scholarships for the autumn. At the sound of footsteps she stood straighter, as she faced the pink-cheeked stranger who opened the door.

"Anson has gone downtown on an errand, so we'll be alone," the stranger said. "I'm Deree Stephens."

"And I'm Abby Gregory."

"You're exactly on time."

They went together through the hall where the face in the portrait stared down at them with the painted eyes that were so like those of Miss Anson Vann. On the porch, near the tea table, Abby touched the shoulder of her seersucker, wishing it were not so tight and hoping the stranger would not notice. She took a seat in a wicker chair, and thought that being here was like being in a cage, with your breath coming tighter. With an effort she sat back, letting her hands fall to her sides.

"I've never seen anything quite like your playing last night," Deree said quietly.

"I like to play," Abby replied. "And I like to win."

"The winning is far from being most important."

Abby touched her dress again.

"Miss Matthis says your camp has a great deal besides sports."

"Of course we do."

"She says the camp must be very beautiful."

Deree eyed Abby gravely.

"The Great Smokies more than live up to what people say about them."

Into the face with the green eyes came a look of superb calm. It seemed to Abby that here on the porch, by some sleight of mind, Deree Stephens managed a transference so that she was no longer in Cape Fear but on a mountain staring at misty ranges. Somehow Abby, too, had a place on the mountain that in her own mind was just exactly as it had been long ago on the picture post card sent back home to her by her mother from the hills.

"We have our own lake," Deree was saying. "Sapphire—with the purple shadow of Old Stone Face hanging over the water."

Abby began to see the shadow.

"A waterfall," Deree went on. "And lilies on the lake."

"It sounds perfect."

"It is perfect." She seemed to be addressing someone private to herself and more important than her companion. "Mornings of memorable pomp!" And coming back to Abby. "Do you think you would like to come to our camp?"

"More than anything in the world."

"Since seeing you play last night, I've been thinking of you as a scholarship girl." Deree touched the table with her finger. "I hear you've done well at school."

"Miss Matthis has spent a lot of time with me."

Deree's eyelids flickered.

"She tells me you read a great deal."

"I like poetry best." Abby could not conceal an anxious self-consciousness. "That was Wordsworth about the 'memorable pomp,' wasn't it?"

"So you knew." The other spoke in a rush of words that seemed unexpected even to herself. "I think we can use a girl like you at Green Leaf."

"About the fees." Abby bent her head. "Are they high?"

"Your scholarship will take care of them," Deree replied graciously.

To her surprise Abby heard herself sounding very like her father.

"I wouldn't want any favors."

"Oh, you'll have work to do. Gee Gee will find you something."

"Gee Gee?"

"You'll meet her. She's our—well, our captain of sports at camp. But suppose we leave sports out of it as far as you're concerned. We'll do it this way. In the cabins where the girls sleep we have no electric lights. The campers pick up their lanterns at Sky House at night and take them down the paths to their huts. It's a custom at Green Leaf." She bent toward Abby as if to throw a cord toward her. "Would you like to be our lantern keeper?"

It sounded so much like being a vestal virgin that one part of Abby wanted to laugh out loud. But her eyes, watching Deree, were sober.

"I suppose I'd like it."

Sitting like a statue in the wicker chair, Deree did not seem to notice the reply. She did not seem to notice at all.

"I'll need clothes," Abby said.

The other came back to her.

"We have our own outfitters in New York."

"Will the clothes—cost much?"

"I think we can arrange that." Deree pursed her lips. "My daughter Lisa has clothes she won't be wearing. I just ordered everything new for her. I'll send them along to you." She settled deeper into her chair. "They tell me your mother is dead."

"She died four years ago."

Deree did not go on with it and Abby was glad of that.

"Do you think your father will be pleased about the camp?"

"I think so."

"Should I see him before I leave?"

"He's working this morning. Later, he's going out of town with some plants."

"I'll write to him, then."

"When do I come to Green Leaf?"

"We open July 1. Suppose you come a day early— some of the girls do—to get acquainted with your lanterns."

As Deree stood up, Abby stood beside her, knowing

for certain that she was going to the camp and never doubting it afterward. Everything was just beginning and more perfect than had seemed possible. Then, all of a sudden, the basket furniture began to close in on her again—just a little, but it was somehow frightening. She touched the chair as if to push it away.

"You'll be meeting Emmy Vann, Anson's niece from Charleston," Deree said. "Anson will be disappointed at not having seen you."

As they went through the hall Abby glanced at the portrait from which the painted eyes still stared at her. At the door she turned to Deree, noticing for the first time that the other's eyes were like glass which reflects but does not see. The unmoving depths brought her a very real sense of bewilderment. But in the sunlight of the porch her confusion disappeared.

"I'll be at Green Leaf exactly on time," Abby said nervously.

In farewell, Deree took Abby's hand in her own, holding it as if it were the hand of a doll just come alive. Abby saw slim fingers with the half moon of the nails. On one finger a star sapphire in a ring of white gold caught the sunlight and her eye. The ring and the white hand framed themselves sharply in her mind.

"We'll meet you in Flat Rock station," Deree said.

With the words, a dart of pleasure caught at the nape of Abby's neck, but in the same moment, hating a sense of being held without volition, she wanted to break violently away. When she freed her hand, the other did not seem to notice any more than she had noticed the hesitancy of a little while ago about wanting to be the Green Leaf lantern keeper.

"Till June," Deree said.

Abby took with her down the street a sensation of flying, of running, of flinging herself high into the air after a goal that no other person could reach. In some way she did not understand the thought of going to the camp was more exciting than anything had ever been before. It was like coming suddenly upon some land so rare that until now you had hardly even dared to dream of such a place. It was like being given a passport to the country of the heart and permitting you to make it—by some fabulous dream—your own.

FIVE

Jim Brandon sent the Ford along the highway that went through the outskirts of Cape Fear to the country club where the dance was being held. He drove with the ease that comes of not having to concentrate on what you are doing, or at least not having to worry about concentration. In every movement of his hand on the wheel was the hard grace that had drawn Abby toward him from the moment of meeting when he moved to Cape Fear two years before.

From her place beside him she watched the shadows of houses and the shadows of trees that stood near them. Each mile was familiar, with this first open field over there one known since she could remember. But for all that, this was a different landscape from the one of the morning, of the talk with Deree Stephens, and the walk that had come afterward, past the Turtle Fountain and along the familiar streets toward home.

Abby smoothed the dress that lay in too-gauzy folds about the high-heeled sandals bought for the dance. Thinking once more of the music that would soon be starting, of the boys in their dark jackets and the girls in glittering dresses, she wished desperately for the game of last night and the freedom it had brought. Once she almost spoke to Jim about it and then unconsciously snuggled deeper into the seat.

He drove along the highway very quietly, held in check by the same stillness that sometimes came over him at the beach when he sat watching the summer ocean twist against the shore, then retreat down the dark sand to rise again with the next wave. His was a stillness frightening because of the action it held in bond, but even in drawing away from him, Abby longed for a time when the action would no longer frighten her.

Then she would hold him close—close—— It came to her suddenly that this summer she would not be with Jim at all.

"You look different tonight," he said, pulling the car to a stop in the pine grove near the club, turning so that his eyes met hers, with the dark like a screen between them. "More grown up."

"I don't feel grown up."

There in the pine grove, watching his face, she thought how like her father he had sounded a moment ago, half pretending his words and half something else. She thought, too, of the frown that had come on her father's face this afternoon when she told him the news about the camp. She would not tell Jim about the camp. Not yet. Wait until after the dance, in the driveway at home, when she was so close to him that it would not seem possible ever to be separate again.

Then Abby spoke suddenly, saying what she had not intended to say.

"Mrs. Stephens is one of the prettiest persons I ever saw."

"Who is Mrs. Stephens?"

"A friend of Miss Anson Vann."

"What has she got to do with us?"

Abby swallowed hard.

"Mrs. Stephens has a camp in the mountains and I'm going there this summer."

He spoke at last.

"We were going to have a house party this summer. Go swimming. Take pictures of the ponies on the outer banks."

"I'll be home by September."

"That's a long time."

"I know it is. But I've got to go to this camp, Jim."

"Why?"

"I don't know yet myself. But I'm going and nobody can stop me."

"Anybody's got to know why he wants to go to a place," he said.

"Maybe I want to go to find out why."

He gripped the wheel hard with his hands.

"That's a crazy reason."

"I didn't say it wasn't."

He looked at her questioningly.

"Is it Miss Matthis?"

"It's my own idea."

Jim was harsher now.

"You'll be different when you come back."

He pulled the car to a stop in the driveway where the lights from the dance floor glittered through the pines and music filled the air. Inside the club, already dancing, were girls from the houses on Market Way. Dancing in the circle of Jim's arms, she would still somehow be apart and alien from them, one who comes from a different, leaner country and still has miles to go. But in the journey to the camp this summer the gap between her and the dancers would begin to close.

"A camp like that might be a good place for people like the Vann crowd," he said. "But not for us."

"They're no different from us."

"Oh, yes, they are."

"But how?"

"They don't want the same things we do, Abby. They're just not our kind."

She turned to him, her face wearing a look of having a secret and at the same time of begging a favor. Who are my kind, she wondered. What am I? What is my name? If Jim knew, could he tell her? But he really did not know. Still, when he was with her the loneliness got pushed further away. Abby made a gesture of moving closer to him and then drew back. There in the darkness, smoothing her long dress, she had a sudden sense of the loneliness coming again, like the wind in the trees overhead.

"Abby," he said suddenly, "you're beautiful. Like one of your father's flowers. One of these days you'll believe me, and then——"

The wind came more strongly, with the trees a barrier between the car and the club, between the car and any place at all. Jim breathed quickly as he took Abby in his arms, with the closeness of their bodies to each other pushing the loneliness to nothing at last. This is what I've wanted, she thought. This was what she had been waiting for without understanding the waiting. Then, all of a sudden, the fear came.

"Let me go, Jim . . . please. Let me go!"

When she pushed his hand from her bare breast he did not speak. But there in the dark the sense of his nearness was stronger than before and somehow more frightening, like the nearness of an animal. She opened the door, and moved from the car with Jim behind her. As they walked down the path toward the lights of the club Abby had a sudden suspicion that a moment of deciding had got past her. Beyond it lay the fear of having lost a time to be.

SIX

In the bedroom, that last day at the farm, the green-dark shadows that meant traintime must be near moved across the floor to the bed where the suitcase lay open. As she packed, Abby's face had a quiet in it, but if you had looked hard you would have seen in her eyes the intensity of a traveler who is ready to move by some western compass toward ranges where not a camp but a desire lies waiting for her.

Suddenly conscious that the shadows had blotted themselves into the floor, she folded a blouse and dropped it into the suitcase on the bed. That was the last of the clothes except the sweater Jim had given her, and in remembering his wary disapproval when he handed her the present, she was reminded again of her father. She picked up the sweater, stared for a moment at its dark green strands, then dropped it into the suitcase and snapped the lock shut as if forever.

On her way downstairs she went slowly but with the air of following someone who goes faster and does not intend to pause or rest. In the living room near the grandfather's clock that had belonged to her mother she put her suitcase on the floor and gazed into a time not shown on the hands of any clock. When her aunt came through the kitchen door to say good-by, Abby hardly saw the familiar figure.

"So you're ready," Janie said.

"I'm ready. Maybe we'd better call Henry."

"He's gone."

"Gone?"

"He went into town on the truck with a load of plants. He'll meet you at the station."

"Then I'll call Father," Abby said.

At that moment, almost as if someone had called him,

Karl Gregory turned away from the crotons he was bagging in the north field and walked toward the house. He came with his hands swinging loosely at his sides, leaving little patches of dirt on the blue serge of his trousers. In the driveway near the house he paused for a glance at the Cape jessamine bushes Abby's mother had helped him plant there the spring before Henry was born.

A long time ago, that year of the planting. Or seemed to be. A long time, another one, with all of them at the farm knowing she would not be here again, and yet with some of them expecting her the way you do with the dead. Sometimes, in the late part of a day, it was easy to see a remembered image or hear the echo of words falling like leaves from the maple tree. That sense of somebody being on the way back rises sharply. Then another day it all changes to become as though the dead had never been alive at all.

"I'll see about your luggage," her father said as he came into the living room.

He went on up the stairs to the bedroom, leaving Abby standing by her aunt. For a moment they were swathed in the silence that comes when too much is remembered and none of it can be spoken, not in the time just before a departure or in any other time. When Janie did speak it was in a stitched-down voice she used to keep her emotions sewed up inside of her.

"Well—it really is time for you to go." And with a

sudden flurry of insecurity, "You let me know if those clothes I made over for you are all right."

"They'll be right."

In the reply lay the cramping hold that always came when it seemed to Abby that she might or would be in the slightest way different from the girls who were waiting for her at the camp in the hills. As she kissed her aunt, and then kissed her again, she looked suddenly older than her sixteen years, and in another way frighteningly like a child. Janie smoothed the collar of the dress bought for the journey.

"Have a good summer, Abby."

Her father came down the stairs with the bag and Abby followed him through the door and across the yard to the car. As they started out, she sat back in the seat beside him, remembering the many times of feeling close to him and knowing that it would never be quite the same again as it had been before that morning in the spring with Deree Stephens. He spoke to her as they turned into Market Way, leaving the outskirts of the town behind them.

"Look," he said. "They got the bridge up."

Far down, past the plaza, the steel fang of the new drawbridge of which he was so proud climbed up against a low-country sky of swamp-trumpet green that seemed more sea than air. Behind the flat arm of the span the tips of the trees above the marshes formed a fine iron tracery. Along the river with its scuffling gulls a strong tide flung itself toward the sea thirty miles away.

"Fine bridge," he said suddenly. "Fine place, Cape Fear. Going away to the mountains still seems to me like wasting a summer."

"I want to go," Abby replied. "I want to be with Mrs. Stephens."

"You can't count on people like her." He shook his head. "A place like that camp. Too high up. Too rich."

At the station, as he thrust the Ford into a parking place, Abby started to answer him and then let the words die in her throat. She got out of the car and stood waiting at the curb while he lifted the luggage from the rear seat and gave it to a porter. Pretending to watch, she saw through her father into the mind's eye country Deree Stephens had created for her last spring. This was a land where tumbling ranges held valleys, and in the land-cups lakes lay like stars. There were not any words for a country like that.

"Let's go," Karl said.

A tide of people went with them toward the train, a boy with bucket-big eyes and an old lady starting out for Charleston with a Cape jessamine on her shoulder. As she walked with the others, Abby was filled with a hard restlessness for a new landscape with its hope of something she had been seeking since her mother's death, had stopped trying to find in Cape Fear, had given up

hope of finding at all, only since springtime to seek it
again. These were the waters you see in dream, weep for
in waking, and lie down to seek again.

"Looking for somebody?" her father asked.

She thought of Jim, but she spoke of her brother.

"For Henry."

"He's meeting us under the shed."

As her father beckoned her toward the corridor, she
turned again, as if still searching, before entering the
station.

SEVEN

THE railroad station in Cape Fear looked like
the end of the line, which it was. The corridor from the
main Shore Road offices to the ticket gate ran like a
cave of smudges and cinders demanding that all who
enter here abandon hope. On the far side of the ticket
gate, big concrete blocks jammed like tombstones at the
tracks' end suggested that this was a place at which people arrived but from which they never departed. Even
the south-bound train seemed clamped to the rails. On
Track One its engine puffed in broken breaths as if du-

bious whether the scheduled departure would actually take place.

Nothing of the station in Cape Fear seemed ever to have been new. Under the shed the plaque for those who fell in the Civil War had not as yet been replaced by a shaft in honor of those who died in 1918. Along the runway the air itself seemed infected, heated by a summer that was still to come, warm and sticky in the June dusk. The Negroes who walked toward the Jim Crow car wore fatigue as their badge. The old lady with the Cape jessamine shook her finger at a laggard porter but shook it slowly, for nobody here ever would be in a hurry.

"I wonder what happened to Henry," Abby said.

"He'll be along," her father replied.

"Sometimes he forgets."

"Not this time."

As her father paused to light his cigar, the snap of the match was echoed in the snap of the elastic band Mr. Pratt, the conductor, bounced against a sheaf of papers as he came toward them along the runway. The conductor had the ferret eye of someone who knows his destination exactly and how long it will take for him to get there. But in twirling his watch chain against his blue vest he spoke to Karl with words so unhurried that they seemed to belie the fact that he had any destination at all.

"Where's Abby going?"

"She's spending the summer at a camp in the mountains near Flat Rock," Karl replied. "You take good care of her for me."

"I'll get her to Flat Rock for you," the conductor replied dryly as he turned away. "And get her home."

"Where's Henry?" Abby asked again.

Her father jerked his thumb toward the gate and from it along the runway came a nine-year-old boy. He came fast, as if the concrete walk under his feet were a lava field that had to be skipped over. His denims fitted tightly but his shirt hung loosely from his shoulders. The pale straw-colored hair, cut short like a convict's, gave him a false air of amazement and set up in Abby a corresponding amazement that he should be alive at all. For her his face would always be the one that had belonged to her mother.

"Will you write to me?" Henry asked.

"Of course."

"Will you write to Jim?"

"Did he tell you to ask me?"

As if to come between them, Karl dropped a hand on Abby's shoulder.

"I may come by the camp for a visit with you," he said. "They're saving me some plants at the Pisgah nursery. I'll take the old road into Flat Rock—the one your mother and I took a long time ago."

The words clanged in her head as the bell announcing the near moment of the train's departure began to ring. On the track the engine shivered, as if coming at last to the time of decision. Karl bent toward his daughter, his face angular in shadow. As he held her, touching her lips, the stubble of his beard was like wire against her cheek. In the embrace she moved uneasily, almost as if the kiss were a stigma instead of a mark of affection.

"Good-by," he said. And Henry picked up the words.

Karl turned away and turned back again, unable to make up his mind whether to stay until the train left the station or go now and have done with it. But when Henry jerked at the arm of his coat he went along under the shed. Abby had a last glimpse of him going along into the dusk, moving toward the gate, dwindling, and Henry beside him dwindling, until at last they were no more than matchstick forms disappearing down the cavernous gray corridor that dissolved into the summer night.

She turned away then, climbing the steps into the Pullman, and blinking her eyes against a yellow light that glowed as if formed by gas rather than by filament and spark. As the train bumped at last into movement she looked up to find Mr. Pratt at her side, and, seeing him, felt a strong aversion. If the conductor did not exist, or if she did not exist in relationship to him, then perhaps Cape Fear would really be in the past, sealed up and gone. But even in the moment of aversion she was overcome with the futility of trying to escape someone who is not so much a person in himself as part of what you can never really leave.

"If you're hungry," he said affably, "we got a diner up ahead."

"I'm not hungry."

"If you change your mind, don't wait around too long. The diner closes soon. It won't open again until in the morning after we've picked up the passengers from Charleston."

"Maybe later," Abby said.

He began to pick his way over the speckled dust green of the Pullman carpet, but turned again.

"We got an Emmy Vann coming on at Charleston," he said. "Kin to the Vanns at home, maybe?"

"Is she getting off at Flat Rock?"

"Yep."

"Miss Anson Vann's niece, Emmy, is going to the same camp I am."

"What camp is that?"

"Green Leaf."

"So you're going to Green Leaf." The conductor shook his head. "They tell me it's a place for rich people."

"It's a fine place," Abby replied. "And I have a scholarship."

He left her to move forward into his world of ticket stubs and of dining cars that would soon be closed until morning. Abby stared through the dusk at the fugitive shapes of pines big in the fields, and moved forward again into the time that lay ahead. In other cars, other travelers would be lost in terraced light instead of being

shut up in an almost-empty Pullman that had the odor
of Cape Fear. But at last she was moving toward the
world of the camp, luminous and beguiling, that would
soon be everywhere. She came unwillingly into the present as the face of the porter moved into focus before her.

"Mr. Pratt gave you a new berth," he said. "In this
one you won't hear the wheels."

His image faded as the train began to slow down for
a wraith of a town with cardboard buildings dimly lit on
a tired street beside an endless line of track. It seemed to
Abby that the little box of a station sliding by held mul-
tiple images that were best drowned in forgetfulness. On
that corner, under a street lamp that threw out less light
than the enveloping dark, she saw a girl's figure that
might have been her own. As the train began to gather
speed again, tunneling its way through the night, she
stood up, inching forward from a Cape Fear that would
never be far enough away.

EIGHT

IN THE light of morning Abby sat up and opened
the suitcase, looking past the sweater Jim had given her
as if it were not there. When she closed the traveling bag

it was with the same final snap given the lock yesterday at the farm. She began to dress. She took clothes from a hanger and thrust her arm into the sleeve of a blouse. The gleam of the watch on her wrist brought a sudden moment of surprise at having gone so far from home in the arc of hours that had formed since last night.

With the gesture of a person coming out of the dark, she thrust the curtains of the berth apart and stood straight in the aisle. On the window across the way a small streak of dirt for a moment obstructed her vision of the world outside, then the scene came clear. She looked into a country of dreams and smoke, a land of hills and heights, a tree leaning sidewise in the split of a boulder. At the door of the dressing room she steadied herself before going inside.

Before a mirror sat a girl who must be about as old as herself, a not tall-looking girl with faint freckles on her nose and a smile on the curve of her lips. At Abby's entrance the stranger swung around on the stool, holding her lipstick as if it were a question mark. Neither of them spoke until at last Abby's good morning came tentatively. The girl at the mirror smiled in return.

"Not much room in here," she said. "But I've almost finished trying to make over my face."

"Not many passengers," Abby said.

"There never are many from Charleston," the other replied.

"You came from there?"

"Yes."

Abby spoke hesitantly.

"Would you be Emmy Vann?"

"Yes." Recognition began to replace curiosity in the other's eyes. "I decided to come along to Green Leaf a day early."

"My name's Abby Gregory." Her eyes, darkly intent, were unsure of the reaction the name would bring. "I'm from Cape Fear and I'm on my way to camp, too."

"Of course. My aunt's been writing me about you." Emmy gestured toward the stool across from her. "Won't you sit down? Still plenty of time. We'll be late getting into Flat Rock."

Abby sat down, glancing at the girl again, conscious of painted fingernails, fuchsia lips, and of the casual costliness of the dress the other wore. Her thoughts went inevitably back to the party last spring at the country club after the basketball game. She remembered the too-gauzy dress, cut low on the shoulders, with the folds of the skirt bringing discomfort as she danced. From Emmy Vann she caught a whiff of the perfume that belonged to the country club.

"Have you been to Green Leaf before?" Emmy asked.

Abby shook her head.

"How far is it?"

"It's about twelve miles from Flat Rock."

"Do we drive from there?"

"Mr. Mac—I guess you'd call him the caretaker at

Green Leaf—takes us over to the camp. The scenery's
really something to see."

"Mrs. Stephens told me about it."

"Did she talk a lot about the camp?" Emmy asked.

"She told me about its—memorable pomp."

The other threw back her head in quick laughter.

"I'm sorry," she said, aware of Abby's startled face.
"It's amusing, even though the country is every bit as
beautiful as she says it is." She went on casually. "You
must have impressed Deree when she saw you last spring
at Aunt Anson's. You have a scholarship for Green Leaf,
haven't you?"

Abby nodded.

"Deree saw you play basketball?"

"The last game of the year," Abby replied. "The next
day I went to see Mrs. Stephens at your aunt's. She arranged for me to come to the camp."

"So you'll be helping with sports?"

"No."

"But why not?"

"I'm not quite old enough to be a counselor so I'm
just going to be a camper."

"Will you be doing any kind of work at all?"

"I'm going to take care of the lanterns."

"A strange scholarship," Emmy remarked.

Abby's eyes went dark.

"I'd better have some breakfast," she said.

"I've had my breakfast." Emmy's smile was like an invitation. "But I'd like coffee."

In the dining car, a waiter gestured them to a table. Outside of the window lay the hills. No intrusion of dull fields, of level pine tops, or of a flat-faced river sliding into the sea past the soggy marshes of remembrance. Across from Emmy Vann, Abby suddenly smiled, wondering how it could happen that you could be homesick and happy at the same time.

NINE

BEFORE very long the train that would come into Flat Rock again, bringing more campers to Green Leaf, would pull into the bare mountain station. But now, in the early morning, as Abby lay on the cot assigned to her, there was only the stillness that had fallen down in the night and suffocated the earth over which it lay. No birds sang, and not even a frog croaked from the lake shore. In pushing the blankets away from her body, she had the sense of rolling away a cover of silence.

Abby got to her feet, and went to the hangers that held the camp clothes brought down from Tip Top

Lodge last night, with Deree walking beside her, pausing to point at Old Stone Face and at the lake lying beneath it fringed with cabins. Beyond them had been the height of Sky House, its dining room, and still farther, the stone chimney of Fir Lodge. Last night, as Deree had pointed to the buildings and the hills, they and the secondhand clothes under her arm had seemed to Abby to have already become her own.

But now, in the still loneliness of the morning, the camp was like an untaken city, and these clothes that had belonged to Deree's daughter Lisa still seemed to belong to her. Abby picked up a flannel blouse, wondering, as she began to dress, about the girl who had worn it. Before the bureau she looked into the mirror as if half expecting the figure there, as well as its garments, not to be her own. Quickly, she turned away.

A little later, going toward Sky House, she paused on the long slope before the cabin to watch the lake with its dock where rows of canoes, their colors grave in the half light of morning, lay waiting for the people who would bring them alive. From a cove she watched last night's mist clear from the trees as the first line of morning came over the hills to touch the thick leaves at the edge of the shore.

A deer swam silently through the waters, advancing from the far side of the lake, alone, the only creature in the world. Moving steadily in the fog of dawn, it left a little track in the water, small ripples on the still surface.

Nosing toward land, it scrambled into the cove and disappeared, in what seemed to be one moment, into a citadel of green, becoming one with the leaves of the forest.

Its image stayed with Abby as she turned from the lake to go along the path to Sky House for breakfast. The doe—it had to be a doe—still lingered in her mind while she stood on the porch waiting for the breakfast gong, watching the lake again, and still seeing, somehow more clearly now that it was gone, the creature moving through the black, cold waters to climb at last to cover. Turning, she found Emmy beside her, yawning.

"You're up too early," Emmy said.

"Not really," Abby replied. "I'm to see Deree before the others get here, and that won't be long now."

"For me it's too early," Emmy said.

"I couldn't sleep anyway," Abby replied. She looked to the lake shore and the hill up which the doe had gone. "What's over there, Emmy? Behind that range?"

"White Water Mountain." Emmy yawned again.

"What's White Water Mountain?"

"We go up there on the big riding trip. From the cliff you can see a hundred miles into nowhere." She shook her head as they went into the dining room where the table was set for the two of them. "I don't like to see that far." And as she picked up her coffee cup, "Besides, it's too early in the morning to think about it."

Breakfast over, Abby came back to the porch, pausing to look at the mountains again before starting up the path for her talk with Deree. On those ridges, stretching away into the distance, was foliage that still kept the look of an earlier season, so that it was easy to believe it was still April, with summer a long way in the distance. But near Tip Top House, where Deree lived, the fir trees were as bushy as the pines of the low country from which Abby had come. And Deree's living room, bracketed in these firs, had the shadiness that seems to belong with summer.

Once she had adjusted her eyes to the shade she saw a square living room with the sleeping quarters behind it, gray counterpanes on the beds, monogrammed in the dark-green complementary colors of the camp. On the floors were scatter rugs in Mexican shades; on the bookshelf, *The Dialogues of Plato* and Dr. Henry Van Dyke's *The Other Wise Man* kept each other dubious company.

"So you're here."

As Abby came through the door, Deree pushed away papers and got to her feet near the desk. The camp costume she wore gave her an air of rusticity that went well with the room, but her face still kept the delicacy that had impressed Abby so much last spring. There was also authority in her. When she spoke it was with the air of a person who is so accustomed to being obeyed that it would never occur to her that the world may move in reverse.

"One of our counselors has dropped out," she said. "She was going to help with photography."

"Maybe I could take her place," Abby suggested eagerly. "If you have a dark room——"

"You just take care of your lanterns," Deree replied. She added with a smile, "I'd planned a long talk with you this morning but Mr. Mac came over to tell me that the campers got an early start from Flat Rock and will be here any minute. Suppose we go over to the gate to meet them."

They went down the road, past the parking space and the bushy firs, and up a little knoll near a barred gate with *Green Leaf* burned into the wood. When Deree came to a halt at the gate, and stood with the hills as a backdrop, she seemed to Abby to wear the look of dedication that some high priestess of a temple of Diana might have worn as she prepared a sacrificial ritual before an altar in a green grove.

After a moment Mr. Mac, his face like a walnut above his checkered shirt, came down the path to stand at Deree's side. He stood with his hands on his hips, resting easily as men do when it is not important for them to go anywhere or to think about going. Then, after a moment, he stuck his hand into the pocket of his shirt and pulled out a piece of paper, and handed it to Deree.

"They gave it to me in Flat Rock early this morning, so I read it. Lisa's going to be late getting here from New York."

"I'd hoped she would come with the others."

As she watched the camp director, Abby saw that

Deree's fingers were pink-tipped as if to match the wool jacket worn last spring instead of the more somber camp clothes. But the star sapphire was gone. In a way, that made Deree more herself than she had been. Abby put her own fingers against the green sleeve of her camp blouse as if to match them with the fingers of Deree.

"I hear cars on the lake road," the other said.

From far away the sounds of song drifted over the waters, with the honking of the car horns breaking the enchantment of the woods. Watching the paper, Abby thought of Lisa, Deree's daughter, who would soon be on her way to the mother who wanted her here. She turned away from the paper as the first of the line of cars with the drivers borrowed from Neekoma Lodge across the range came into sight.

From these cars the occupants called out to each other and to Deree. The words of the song came clearly now. *Going back—going back—going back to stay till fall— going back—going back—to the best camp of them all.* As a car pulled to a halt, an Indian chief of a woman with wiry, short-cropped hair jumped from the lead car and came across the road to Deree.

From the other cars came girls, tall ones, short ones, swirling toward the gate together, strange in their city clothes, calling names to each other: Ty, Ellie, Betsy, Lissie. Emmy, arriving at last, still yawning, moved among them to take the arm of a young woman in a navy-blue suit whose red hair pushed its way impudently from under a knitted cap that matched the suit. Even in the crowd, the face under the knitted cap had a friendliness more easily apparent than that found in any of the other faces.

"Peg, this is Abby Gregory," Emmy said.

The newcomer gave Abby a smile.

"You're in my cabin."

The counselor turned toward Deree who stood talking with the Indian chief, who must be Gee Gee Stern. Handsome, this one, and as bold, too, as any savage. Now she reached into the pocket of her coat for a silver whistle that hung from a thin chain. The whistle at her mouth, she manufactured a shrill blast that moved out over the lake and bounced back at the camp from the side of a hill on the other shore.

"Go to your cabins," Gee Gee said. "When you get there, change into your camp clothes."

The girls began to move away, dissolving like shadows into the landscape. Before going with the others back down the path toward Tip Top House Deree let the telegram from Lisa flutter to the ground to lie there beside the parked car. Watching the flapping paper, Abby began to wonder what kind of person this Lisa Stephens was—late and not apparently minding it. She came to attention as Gee Gee Stern turned away from Mr. Mac and came briskly toward her.

As she came with her long stride, Abby felt the muscles in her stomach tightening as they did before some difficult contest. Gee Gee Stern was like a Gulliver, with Abby inch-high; or like a captain, who understood that already perhaps some member of his crew—some inch-high Abby Gregory—was plotting to revolt against his discipline.

"Get along to your cabin with the others," Gee Gee said. "You'll be late for assembly!"

TEN

ABBY came half-awake to lie beneath the blankets staring at the faces, innocent in sleep, of the girls with whom she shared this cabin among the leaves. Sara, Bobby, Lissie—all friends. In the time since the camp had opened, almost in the moment of seeing one another's faces, they had moved into an acceptance that made it seem they had been at the camp always instead of for just one week.

Abby turned away from the sleeping campers, and glanced at the rear wall with its schedule for the day, beginning with the exercises that were held each morning before breakfast on the slope near Sky House. The girls, tall ones, short ones, fat ones, and others as alike as if they had been poured from the same mold, would line up on the hill like soldiers. Before these exercises would come the long trill of the bugle blown by Mr. Mac in his cabin, a signal that the night was over and the activities of the day would soon begin.

Abby pushed back her pillow, lying with her hands under her arms, staring now at Freddie Daniels whose picture, brought from Louisville by Peg, and as much a part of the cabin as the girls themselves, stared back at her from the dresser. Freddie had ears that were set close to his head like Jim's. I wonder where Jim is now, at this moment, she thought, and then forgot him as the notes of reveille split the air.

"I dreamed I was chosen for the White Water trip," Bobby said, rubbing a hand across her forehead.

The others, too, moving away from cots that had until now sagged under their sleeping shapes, came unwillingly from dream to morning. At the sound of Gee Gee's whistle from the porch of Sky House they left the cabin, still half-drowned in the subterranean world of sleep, to go along the lake path with its mists and water lilies to the game court for the exercises.

Abby went with the others, falling silently into step beside Ida, one of the riding counselors, who was on duty for the exercises this morning. A tall woman with a chalk-dust face, who walked by some pushing force, as if each step were an effort, Ida seemed to be a person who had a great deal farther to go than from the cabin to the game court. Gee Gee Stern, stiff as a master of a vessel, stood as if on a bridge deck waiting for a lifeboat drill, called out of deference to future necessity, to begin.

"The exercises make me ill," Ida said.

"They make me want to laugh," Abby replied. "All of us spread out on the hill—choo-chooing away like a lot of fake locomotives."

The counselor came to a stop, looking at Abby strangely.

"You don't want to get in trouble, Abby?"

"No—no, of course not."

"Then I'd keep quiet if I were you," Ida said. "About the exercises, and about anything else that belongs to Gee Gee."

"But I don't see . . ."

Ida spoke again as she turned away. "Just be glad for a warning."

After breakfast was over the girls—some of them still sleepy—came to the porch of Sky House, pausing for a moment before moving on again to take part in the morning sports hour that would end when it was time for the assembly talk that Deree gave each day. As Abby turned away from the porch rail to go back to her cabin and dress for riding, Gee Gee came through the dining room door to call out to her in high, clear words that had a snap behind the lightness.

"Abby—just a minute."

As Abby turned to face the tall figure with the bandana tight around her head, she felt a reasonless desire to laugh with a dislike lying behind it. It was not just a response of the moment. On that first day of the sharp command to get to her cabin, and in the days that had gone by since, she had felt wary of Gee Gee and somehow afraid. Facing her, Abby stood in the attitude of a raw recruit called too quickly to attention.

"I've been wanting to talk with you," Gee Gee said. "Before long we're going to be needing some new lantern shades."

So it was nothing. A wind that was not there. So it was nothing at all.

"We've decided to send you over to the Ridge Store in Flat Rock the next time Mac makes the trip. You can pick the shades up then."

She stepped away from Abby to touch the banister rail with a brown finger and stare beyond it at the mountain. Over the top of Old Stone Face came a trail of clouds, moving toward the lake with its still-black waters untouched by wind. It was as if, in watching, Gee Gee offered the clouds an invitation in her black, hard eyes.

"Do you like being at camp?" she asked suddenly.

"Very much."

"This is quite a change for a girl like you, isn't it?"

"I suppose so."

"We're glad you like Green Leaf," Gee Gee went on. "And we want to like you."

"I don't know what you mean."

"You"—the other touched her bandana with a brown finger—"like to go your own way, don't you?"

"My own way?"

"The morning exercises are not performed for your amusement," Gee Gee snapped.

"I'm not amused."

"You seem to be."

"I do like to laugh. At home——"

"This isn't home," Gee Gee replied. "Here you are just one of a group of seventy girls. And one who has a lot to learn."

Abby took a quick, hard breath. The dislike of a little while ago came again, more strongly, changing the day around her, blackening the cliff of the mountain and the lake that lay under it. She felt a real hatred of this woman in front of her, almost as if it would be pleasant to get into a tussle and see who would be the victor. But when Gee Gee spoke again the hatred was replaced by the need to snap to attention.

"I've changed your swimming hour," she said. "Riding at three this afternoon. Swimming this morning at ten." She looked at Abby appraisingly. "Lisa Stephens will be in charge."

"So she's here."

Gee Gee shaded her eyes with her hand to look toward the dock where the first canoe group was gathering and the life raft was being pushed to its place through a patch of lilies. No doubt about who was really in charge here. The lake, the campers, and even the frogs on the lilies were Gee Gee's for the shouting. Again Abby felt the dislike, blacker and more bitter than before.

"If you're serious about wanting to belong at Green Leaf," Gee Gee said, "you might watch Lisa."

"I'll watch her, if that's what you want." Abby flushed as she turned away.

ELEVEN

AFTER the clouds of the morning had begun to go, Abby went past the game court where contests would be held during Festival Week, still a long time away, and along the line of cabins to dress for swimming. On the steps of her cabin sat Emmy, wearing a blue bandana as if in caricature of Gee Gee, languidly polishing her riding boots. Watching, and reminded again of the dislike of Gee Gee that had come over her on the porch, Abby began to wonder if there had really been a wind, after all.

"You'd better start getting ready for riding," Emmy said.

"I won't be going to the ring this morning."

"Why not?"

"Gee Gee changed my schedule."

"Cleaning those lanterns again?"

"No—swimming." Abby sat down on the step. "Lisa Stephens will be on the dock." She reached over to pick a leaf from a laurel bush. "What's this Lisa like?"

"Why do you want to know?"

"I'm just curious."

"Who's been talking to you about her?"

"Gee Gee."

"What did she tell you?"

"To watch her. To try to be like her, I suppose."

Emmy held up a boot and squinted at it, speaking in Deree's own voice.

" 'You, Abby Gregory, have been chosen———' "

Abby let the laurel leaf fall to the ground.

"Oh, stop it."

"Maybe she just told you to watch her because Lisa is Deree's daughter."

"Really, Emmy. What kind of person is she?"

"Lisa is the kind of person who can do anything." Emmy was suddenly sober. "And sometimes does, or so Larry says."

"Who's Larry?"

"Her brother. He's taking pre-med at Columbia."

"Do you know him?"

"I met him in New York last year when Aunt Anson took me for a visit during the holidays."

Abby looked at Emmy with a flicker of envy.

"You like this Larry?" she asked. And making her own reply. "You *do* like him."

"Of course I do." Emmy smiled at her. "He'll be coming to camp before long. Maybe you can learn from him about Lisa."

As Emmy turned to go into the cabin Abby called out to her.

"What are you really trying to tell me about Lisa?"

"Maybe I'm trying to say that you shouldn't believe everything you hear." Emmy's eyes became evasive.

"Go on."

The other glanced down the slope toward the water lilies lying on the lake.

"Lisa's lovely," she said.

She seemed about to say more, then, changing her mind, took the riding boots from the ledge beside her and went into the cabin.

TWELVE

In her own cabin Abby began to dress for the swimming hour, pulling on a yellow bathing suit that was outrageously gay in contrast to the subdued grays and greens of the camp clothes. Placing the blouse that had belonged to Lisa Stephens on the bed beside the new sweater, she found her swimming cap and retraced her steps down the line of cabins, walking along the lake path on her toes to keep the pebbles from bruising the tender soles of her feet.

On the dock, where the swimmers for the hour now gone were climbing the ladder from the pen, or taking last dives from the high board, Abby paused to stare at a girl who was calling out in a clear voice to a belated swimmer. The voice had a ripple in it, and a trace of laughter. The face and figure seemed to be an exact accompaniment to the voice. Tall, with a sensuous fullness of the body, this girl stood, her head bright in the sun above her tight bathing suit, waiting with a half-indulgent air for the last of the swimmers to depart.

"About time for the new crowd!" she called.

In the words were a pride and a certainty that was more impressive than the pride. Proud and insolent, this one, even in the movement of the hand that was so like Deree's—and on this pointing finger the star sapphire of last spring, seeming to catch its color from the waters of the lake. To conceal a growing uncertainty, Abby turned and dived from the dock into clear, cool water that in the sunlight was a pool in which to drown an unwanted remembrance.

She swam forward, freed of the impact of Lisa by the impact of the lake and yet somehow conscious of a loneliness deeper than any felt since she had come to the camp. Circling the float that was anchored near the far lily pads, she climbed to the rubber mat on the dock and began to shake beads of water from her face. For a long time she sat staring at the mountains with the words Jim had whispered last spring coming back to her. *You're beautiful, Abby, like one of your father's flowers. One of these nights you'll believe me, and then*—— To love, to be loved. A proud person like Lisa Stephens would know all about that. As she watched the face, she was shorn for the second time that day of a dignity she had never even possessed enough to be able to pretend it belonged to her.

With the swimming hour over, one last diver arched from the board, sliding almost soundlessly into the lake, then emerging to come by easy crawl to the dock. From the other side of the board Lisa came indolently, pausing at last to stare down at the figure in the yellow bathing suit. She spoke as if careless whether her words reached Abby, careless whether the other existed at all. But the sting was there.

"What kind of stroke were you using to go to the float?" she asked.

"I got there and back, didn't I?" Abby said.

She wanted desperately to be removed to some far-away place that would separate her forever from the stare of this person. She slid into the water, and swam again to the float but not so fast as before. When she came back to climb up the slick ladder to the mat, Lisa was still standing by the diving board giving instructions to a last swimmer.

"You turn the palm, letting it lie in the water. Try it when we have class in the morning."

She sounded as if the process, or any process for that matter, was too simple to have to be explained. Abby pretended to look at the lilies, and kept on pretending until only the two of them were left alone on the dock. I am nobody, she was thinking. Nobody at all. As she turned at last to go, Lisa called out to her.

"Are you going to the riding ring?"

"Not till later."

She stared at the figure across from her, trembling as if afraid. For a moment Lisa seemed about to give an order, to clip it out of her mouth as Gee Gee Stern might have clipped a command. Slender, dark, Abby faced her. After a time, when Lisa reached down to touch a line that would secure a sailing canoe closer to the dock, Abby put out a hand to help.

"I ride no better than I swim," she said.

When Lisa laughed it was as though they had been laughing together all the time.

"Is my swimming really so bad?" Abby asked.

"A hopeless stroke," Lisa replied. "But I'll soon teach you a good one."

The sun, hot on the face of the mountains above the riding ring, filtered down through a screen of leaves. It cast a shadow over scraggly daisies that grew near the shed where Mr. Mac was helping saddle the horses that Ida, had she been here, would have had ready an hour ago for the afternoon ride. At the rail, where the beginners waited, there was the smell of straw, of rank sweat, and of the firs near the shed. Across the meadow was the long line of mountains, and the tallest of them White Water.

Ty Barnet, lingering from the advanced class, wiped her face that somehow always seemed oily, and called out to Sara.

"You weren't doing too well with that singlefoot."

"Everybody can't ride as well as you," Sara replied pleasantly.

Ty giggled.

"Ida seems to think they can."

Chewing a last bite of apple, Emmy spoke to Ty.

"What's wrong with Ida today? Bussi's having to take her place again."

"Search me," Ty said. "I guess she's just the kind who's never right."

"Gee Gee won't go for that very long," Emmy observed, throwing the apple core away.

"If Ida's really sick, what can you———" Abby interrupted herself as Mr. Mac came from the stable to drop a casual hand on her shoulder.

"You coming with me on the big trip?" he wanted to know.

"White Water?" She could not keep the eagerness out of the words.

He laughed dryly.

"To Flat Rock for the lantern shades."

"Yes—yes, of course."

She turned and walked to the rail where he had tied her horse. In the ring, when instruction began, Bussi James called Emmy to help out for a while. Now the sharp commands—walk, trot, walk again, with Abby handling the reins tentatively, and with Emmy beside her, easy in the saddle, eying the other with open curiosity.

"About Lisa?" Emmy wanted to know. "What did you think of her?"

Abby looked past the riding ring, over the hills to the peak of White Water.

"You were right," she replied at last. "Lisa's lovely."

THIRTEEN

ABBY picked up a can of kerosene and began the task of filling the squat containers with oil from the big tin that stood under the shed near the back porch of Sky House. Before long she would polish each shade with a soft fleece cloth so that the lanterns could be hung again on their hooks, polished and trimmed, ready for the girls to carry them down the paths to the cabins when night came.

As she put the kerosene can on the porch floor, Peg called out to her.

"The mail's here."

The counselor shuffled through the envelopes, separated one, and then seemed to forget that there were others. As she stared at the oblong of paper, Peg moved into a space outside of the camp. Glancing up, she spoke with a voice that belonged back in Louisville.

"I already know what's in this letter. Freddie doesn't

want me to stay over at the end of the camp to help
Deree close Green Leaf."

"Will you stay?"

"I halfway promised Deree."

"Then you'll have to stay, won't you?"

"I don't think I can bear to be away from him," Peg
said. Then with a sudden smile, "Oh—a letter for you,
Abby. From Cape Fear."

Abby took the letter, staring at Jim's name scrawled
across the back of the envelope. When Peg had gone
on down the path toward the cabin, Abby sat down on
the edge of the porch still staring. His handwriting somehow belonged to a stranger. What's wrong with me this
morning? she wondered. *I think of you all the time,
Abby. While I'm working, or at the beach, it isn't so bad,
but the nights are rotten. Every time I sleep I dream of
you. The sweater I gave you. When you wear it, remember me.*

On the steps by the lanterns she breathed quickly,
holding the letter too tightly in her hand. For a long moment she sat there, staring up the slope past the scraggly
daisies, as if hunting for an image she would never find.
Then, almost as if choosing this moment by intention,
Lisa rounded the corner of the porch and came toward
the lanterns. Instinctively, Abby shielded the paper in
her hand.

"Still working?"

The derision was there, but not so strong as Abby imagined it to be.

"I'm almost through for the morning," she replied.

"What are you hiding?"

"A letter from home." She put the envelope in her pocket. "At home on our farm I've always worked with my hands."

"Maybe you like it." Lisa laughed lightly. "I'd never choose it myself."

"Have you ever cleaned a lantern?" Abby wanted to know.

"No, and I never will." The other yawned. "Larry took them on one summer."

From the edge of the porch Lisa reached down for a daisy, and shredded it to nothing. The star sapphire— her mother's ring, Abby thought with envy—began to flash in the sun. Suddenly Abby remembered Emmy's words: *Lisa can do anything she wants to do. And sometimes does.* Here, where the daisies were few and scraggly, Lisa was destroying the best one almost as if she had chosen it by instinct. In the mellow sunshine Abby watched the other gravely.

"Emmy says your father's dead," she said.

"Yes." Then with no change of tone: "What else has she been telling you?"

Abby swallowed dryly.

"About your brother—he's coming to camp?"

"Emmy likes him." Lisa gave the words a lightness.

"Will Deree let her see him?"

"Larry's always had his way with Mother." She tossed the daisy stem away. "He really likes Emmy."

"When will he come?"

"Wednesday, I think. Maybe with a friend of his. Men aren't supposed to come into camp until visitors' week, but Jake Dean may stop over with Larry for a night. His people have a summer place over at Cray Lake, and Larry visits him there."

"This—Jake—is he your friend?"

Lisa shrugged indifferently.

"He's just a brute boy from over the hill."

In watching that flower face, and in hearing the words, Abby felt a tenuous but definite sense of relief. Under Lisa's glance she felt that the intimacy of yesterday when they were on the dock had come back to them, with the return bringing a sensation that was like touching fire. In a way I don't understand we are friends, Abby thought. She picked up her polishing rag, got to her feet, and moved to the lanterns again.

"I'd better be finishing up," she said. "It will soon be time for crafts."

"And for swimming." Lisa stretched her arms toward the sky. "You're doing well with that stroke of yours."

She took a step away from Abby toward the door of Sky House, but afterward stood on the porch, her violet eyes holding the watcher in their glance. Abby knew that the other's interest was far more than curiosity. Frightened and pleased at having drawn Lisa back to her, she hung a lantern on the hook as if the morning job were already finished and walked over to stand by the figure near the door.

"Mother tells me you like poetry," Lisa said.

She put a finger to her lips. The hand was frail, not white, but cream-colored in contrast to the bloom of her body. Aware of that body and of the provocative face, Abby had a sudden sense of dizziness. She wondered where the feeling of being stampeded came from and was deeply disturbed that it had come at all.

"My teacher lends me her books," Abby said.

"Somebody in high school?"

"What's wrong with teaching there?"

"Nothing." Lisa shrugged. "Nothing at all." And then, curiously, "What kind of poetry do you like?"

"Any kind." It was not true, but it would have to serve.

"Really? That's impossible."

"I like Robert Frost."

"But he's famous—so famous that everybody likes him."

"I'd like to write a poem as good as—as one of his worst ones. I'd like to be able to say how I feel about a deer that swam across the lake the first morning I came to Green Leaf. Or be able to take a picture of the doe."

Lisa let it go by.

"You should be reading someone of our own time—someone passionate. Perhaps D. H. Lawrence."

The word "passionate" turned into a spear that went straight through Abby. The shock was new and yet as old as remembrance. There on the porch near the other girl Abby again became possessed by that familiar terrifying sense of being torn by forces she had never been able to comprehend or control. It seemed to her that Lisa was fully aware of what was happening. She suspected that her companion was enjoying herself.

"Suppose I read you some Lawrence poems," Lisa said casually.

"When could we read them?"

"We might go out on the lake some afternoon."

"I'd like to."

Lisa's words fell lightly.

"You'd better finish your lanterns. Yes, we'll go on the lake. Lawrence is a wonderful antidote for chimney sweeping."

FOURTEEN

ON THE afternoon of going on the lake with Lisa, Abby sat on the steps of the cabin polishing the riding boots Emmy had loaned her. Glancing at the shining black boots, she began to think of the remark Lisa had made about chimney sweeping. The poem by William Blake, the one Miss Matthis liked—a good poem even if he was famous—had a lot about chimney sweepers in it. Some little black boys who had got locked up in coffins were never going to be able to go free. An angel with a key opened the coffins and sent the children off to wash in a river and shine in the sun. Maybe that would impress Lisa. And I do want to impress her, Abby thought.

From the steps she stared past the lake into trees that were a curtain around the camp. Beyond them were the hidden ranges that held White Water peak. The riding trip to the big mountain was almost here, closer now than it had seemed at the start of the camp it would ever be. Soon the list would be posted on the porch of Sky House, and perhaps her name with the others. She smiled to herself as Bobby Slater called to her from inside the cabin, the voice drifting toward the other voices that came from the lake.

"Are you going to Fir Lodge before supper for the free hour?" Bobby wanted to know.

"I'm going on the lake with Lisa," Abby replied.

She shoved the boots inside the door, and went down the path for the appointed meeting, seeing that face, so like Deree's and yet so much itself, mirrored in the faces of the girls who came along the path that led up the hill to Fir Lodge. Strange about Lisa's face. Last night, when she waked in the dark to the croak of a single frog, it had come at her as if by invitation through the midnight air.

"Hello, Abby."

From the shed where the campers were lifting the brightly colored canoes and dropping them into the lake Ty Barnet, hair too straight above her oily face, called out to Abby. The greeting was drowned in the command that Lisa, walking out under the shed, gave with the ease of a person who always gives commands. As she spoke she pointed to the best canoe, the scarlet one at the end of the line.

"That's ours, Abby—here—slide it this way."

They climbed into the craft, with Abby steadying it against the dock.

"If it's all right with you, Lisa," she said, "I'll paddle."

Lisa nodded, lying back against the leather cushion, trailing her fingers in the water as the craft got underway, Abby sending it through a lily patch into open water. This was a lovely time, with the trees glossy in their heavy summer foliage and with no sound anywhere as they slid forward away from the lake shore and into the open spaces. No sound except the song the girls in the canoes sang as the canoes drifted toward open water.

> *In this real world*
> *Where there is no witchcraft*
> *And golden wishes do not grow on trees,*
> *Our fondest daydreams will be the magic*
> *That brings us back these happy memories.*

They came to a curve in the shore where that first morning Abby had seen the doe moving through the black, cold waters of the lake and disappearing at last into the green forest. The creature had gone with the morning, but now, as she paddled near the remembered place, the image flickered again and more strongly on the leaf screen of her mind. It suddenly seemed to her that she herself became a doe, voyaging through cold waters out of the fog of childishness and dream.

That first day, made for her alone, had come not as some mornings do with a promise and a lull but had seemed to appear full-fledged and in one motion. Under the sky so still, so still, the black, early waters had parted for the doe to make her path through the lake. In

that world of nobody it had seemed to Abby that somehow the moment held a revelation that would become
apparent only in the future but was already in full and
secret being.

That first morning, with pink touching the lake and
sunlight suffusing the heights, had offered a promise of
coming at last to a place where her fears, never to hurt
her again, would vanish like the mists that rose over the
waters and touched the opening lilies. This was like getting out from under cover when you have been afraid
you would never get out again, like getting out from under suffocation and being able to breathe freely.

"What in the world are you thinking about?" Lisa
wanted to know.

"About a doe I saw the morning I came to camp."

"How do you know it was a doe?"

"I didn't," Abby said gravely. "I just wanted it to be
one."

"Let's get away by ourselves to the other end of the
lake," Lisa said quietly. "Nobody takes the trouble to go
as far as the dam."

Near the dam the air was sharp and the silence
seemed sharp, too, after the chatter that had come from
the canoes at the other end of the lake. Drifting now,
Abby let the craft come to rest among closed water lilies,
and sat with the paddle in her hands watching Lisa, who
in turn watched her.

"You paddle well," Lisa said. "In fact, you do every-

thing well. I've known that from the first day, in spite of
your swimming."

She took a book from her pocket, fondling it. As her
companion leaned against the cushions Abby suddenly
felt a pain as dark as the one that sometimes came to her
at night at home when the remembrance of her mother
rose in the darkness to flood the room and her heart. She
bent forward, wanting to tell Lisa she did not know what,
speak to her of what she could not say, sometimes even to
herself. But the other began to read.

> "And still in my nostrils
> The scent of her flesh,
> And still my blind face
> Sought her afresh;
> And still one pulse
> Through the world did thresh.
>
> And the world all whirling
> Round in joy
> Like the dance of a dervish
> Did destroy
> My sense—and reason
> Spun like a toy."

Abby listened, the paddle beginning to trail in the
water like a wing. These words were not only new but
new to her each moment. Lisa had been right about them.
They were an antidote—but for what? They were for
this time—for this minute, too. The sky, the lake, and
the faint voices of the girls in the other canoes got lost
in the words as Lisa began again.

> "But firm at the center
> My heart was found;
> My own to her perfect
> Heartbeat bound,
> Like a magnet's keeper
> Closing the round."

Abby repeated the stanza, staring past Lisa at the lake where the dusk was beginning to hide the white of the waterfall that came off Old Stone Face. Here near the dam, with the world of the camp blocked away, she had a sense of being forced ahead, past country that is known and onto dangerous ground. But there was only the lake, the one star like a lily, and the face of Lisa across from her, as serene as evening.

"You caught all that by hearing it once." Lisa spoke in open admiration. "You do learn fast."

Abby began to tremble. The air on the lake, touched by the nearing night, was cool on her cheeks, but something was burning inside of her. A pleasure more insistent and more intense than any she had ever known before, new and frightening, made every past emotion drop away as if it had never existed. She was doubly afraid and yet understood that having once known this pleasure it would be impossible for her to do without it again.

"Everything you attempt, you do well," Lisa said.

"You told me that before."

"And it's true—believe me, Abby. I know about people."

Abby's eyes held a dark question.

"Do you think Gee Gee knows much about people?"

"She knows how to make them obey her."

"That isn't enough."

"What is enough?" Lisa wanted to know.

Abby spoke slowly, finding the words difficult to say. "My mother used to say that love is."

For a moment it seemed that Lisa was laughing, but when Abby looked again the face of the other was composed. And for all the might-be laughter she was at the border now, here on the lake, of an incredible moment of understanding. She felt that the face sought so often and never found was watching and very close. And Lisa —bending forward from the cushion—what was she saying, and why?

"Love is just a way of playing." She laughed lightly. "But you must know how to pretend it is not a game."

Unable to follow this kind of complexity, Abby sat back, her cheeks hotter than they had been before. A game—a way of pretending. With Jim, it could never be that. It could not and should not be, but those clear eyes in that flower of a face surely must know. Perhaps it was something that could be taught, if you could only be quiet, if you could only wait to learn. Perhaps, in the learning, you could find again what you lost so long ago.

"When did your father die?" Abby asked suddenly.

"Two years ago. The autumn I went up to Alvon as a freshman."

"Do you—still miss him?"

"I feel that he's with me," Lisa said simply.

"Here?"

"Everywhere. At camp. At home in the city." As Lisa trailed her hand in the water the star sapphire shone softly. "He and I had lovely times together."

Abby swallowed hard.

"That's a lovely ring you are wearing."

Lisa looked at the stone.

"Father gave it to Mother. This was their engagement ring."

"So you—loved your father?"

"He was a marvelous man. He and I were so close. He used to take me with him everywhere."   ⋆

"Where is everywhere?"

Lisa shrugged.

"The park—the theater—to the clinic with him sometimes. With Father, Manhattan was always too wonderful."

A city with spangles in its sky dangled before Abby, a dream town hanging down into the lake. A place where you could shake your old self away, become what you wanted to be, what you should be, where you ran fast, fast as you did at home in a game, just for the delight of the running. Lisa Stephens' city, falling down to her from the sky, and one day it would be her own.

"I want to go to New York," she said. "Tell me about it, Lisa."

"There's really nothing to tell." Lisa leaned against the cushions. "When you've spent your life there, you don't have to think about it—you just have it for your own." She laughed softly. "I used to feel that way about our apartment, but these days Gee Gee is all over it."

Abby stabbed the water with her paddle.

"I hate her."

"Why so violent?"

"I have a feeling she's after me."

"She wants you to feel that way. It's her particular compulsion."

"But why—why?"

"Don't ask me." Lisa put the book into her pocket again. "Ask Larry when he gets here. He's the psychiatrist."

"Psychiatrist?"

"I often accuse him of thinking he's one."

"Mr. Mac says we're going to meet Larry in Flat Rock tomorrow."

Lisa nodded.

"I'd go with you but I'm writing some letters for Mother in the morning. It looks as if you'll have to meet him by yourself." She bent forward, letting her hand rest lightly on Abby's arm. "I'd like to be going with you."

With the touch of the light hand again came that strange current of response. It was, as Abby vaguely sensed, far more than a physical thing. Through this hand, resting so lightly on her own, she was made part of a company. It was as if she, too, wore a ring, not yet visible but soon to be apparent to all. The idea was too compelling to combat. And she did not want to combat it.

"Let me see your sapphire," she said.

When Lisa slipped the ring from her finger, Abby brushed the gold against her blouse, giving it a new glossiness. For a long moment she held the ring against the flannel, as if to display it before an unseen audience. As she handed it back to its owner, Lisa spoke in a whisper.

"Why, Abby, you're wearing my blouse."

She leaned still closer, not jarring the balance of the craft in the water. Abby began to sense that she was close to a precarious shifting of the balance of the world, a shifting that might plunge her into colder depths than any she had known before. With the hope of regaining lost ground she put out her hand, grasping the canoe like a person trying to steady himself against a plunge into the water.

"Do you like wearing my clothes?" Lisa asked.

The hills, the sky almost purple now, and the heavy circle of leaves around the lake came together in a composition that was disturbing and yet at the same time brought a supreme moment of happiness. Abby shot to a different level, that was like having been on one level, having climbed up by hard struggle to a new plateau, and having found then that you were still moving to a higher pinnacle. In an instant you saw a different and finer country than you had ever seen before.

"Lisa——"

But whatever Abby had started to say she did not say, for at that moment a big wind came and blew away whatever was inside of her and made her see the scene with an outside eye instead of an inner one, see that this was something she had never been intended for, something that in the atmosphere of the camp seemed somehow sacred and yet was not wrong, maybe, but unreal, feverish, and as fleeting as the lilies that had been everywhere this morning and were now closed up so tight that one thought not of the flowers but only of the long, tangled stems and of the muddy roots that lay under the water.

"You're running away," Lisa said.

"I was just thinking," Abby lied.

"What were you thinking?"

"Nothing."

"Of anyone in particular?"

"No, Lisa, no!"

She held the paddle tight in her hands, moving the canoe with quick strokes toward the dock where the little fleet had already come to port with the other campers. As they slid forward, it seemed to her that there had been much, much more in these moments on the lake than the brief touch, the ring on her finger, and the veiled exchange of words. Beyond these things, or rather beneath them, worked a force that was already holding her in a grasp from which it would be impossible to escape.

> "But firm at the center
> My heart was found;
> My own to her perfect
> Heartbeat bound,
> Like a magnet's keeper,
> Closing the round."

She felt cold and afraid, for it seemed to her that without volition and in a kind of stupid innocence she had managed to be snared in some trap of which she was completely unaware. What frightened her the most was the fact that she did not want to get out of the trap. Somehow even more frightening was the thought that she might want to get out, climbing to freedom through the forests of feeling in the same way the doe that first day on the lake had climbed up the hill through the garden of leaves. Lisa spoke words as soft as the evening air that lay around and over them.

"So you're going to Flat Rock to meet the train. You'll love Larry."

Abby slid the canoe against the dock, staring at the figure lying before her without replying.

FIFTEEN

FIR LODGE sat high on the hillside, so close to the waterfall that after a heavy rain the stream seemed about to broaden out from its bed of rocks and make a channel through the log walls. Outside the windows was the little roar of the water, and above it the stars in a black sky. Inside was a long room with a fireplace in front of which girls stood waiting for the meeting to begin.

Smaller and more intimate than Sky House, the Lodge was used most often for gatherings like this one when Deree intended to talk to the older girls and some of the counselors about the progress that had been made during the part of the camp season that was gone, about the heights lying ahead in the final weeks still to be scaled before Festival Week, with its visitors and pageants, brought with it the end of the season.

Abby walked into the room to the sound of the last lines of the hunting song:

> "A keeper would a-hunting go,
> And over his shoulder he carried a bow,

All for to shoot a merry little doe,
Among the leaves so green . . ."

The singers lounged against the cushions in the window seat, staring at the squares of glass where now and then a bough stirred like a hand. Some sat on the floor looking at the big fire with its red racks of serrated logs. Finding a place beside Emmy Vann, Abby leaned against a wood box and turned her glance toward Deree, who was getting ready for the meeting to which she had summoned them all.

In her big chair made of cherry wood Deree sat staring into the fire as if inspecting some scene remote from the room, but she came quickly back to the campers and to the Lodge when Gee Gee clapped her hands for attention. Watching Gee Gee, the brisk motion, the fine figure, Abby could not resist a grudging admiration. Gee Gee dropped a new log onto the fire and then stood straight, brushing bark from her hands. What Lisa had said was true. This one could get people into the mood of obeying her without even bothering to make a sound.

"Some of you have been at Green Leaf before," Deree began. "Others are new. But by now every one of you must know what the camp stands for." She smiled gravely. "Of course, you counselors have always known."

The counselors who were present nodded like grave birds on a limb. *Fine, upstanding young women, chosen because they are leaders in their own fields.* The catalogue assured you of that. They had the look of early-morning freshness, and of ease. Among them only Ida, the riding counselor, was different. Still in her jodphurs after having come late from the ring, she sat trying to imitate the expression of the others, but her face was strained as if a thin sheet of rubber were somehow holding it in place.

"Gee Gee will have some news of her own for you on the White Water trip," Deree was saying. "As for me, I want to talk a little about the whole camp program."

Gee Gee, her face even more ruddy than usual, nodded permission for Deree to go ahead. Near the fire beside Gee Gee, sitting yogi fashion, Bussi James, who was in charge of riding, twisted a little piece of paper that she had a moment ago taken from her pocket. The girls in the window seats and the counselors on the divan kept staring at Deree with respectful faces. Ida, away from the others, began to stare at the back porch door as if measuring the distance to it.

"It is difficult to believe that we have gone past the middle of our season," Deree was saying. "But the half time is past, and we're moving toward the end."

"Just three more weeks," Ty whispered to Abby. "Then Festival Week."

Deree's face took on the deeper tint the thought of the peak of the camp season always brought to it.

"We will soon begin choosing girls for the play to be given for Visitors' Day. We'll have the people from Neekoma Lodge. And they'll stay through until Fire Night."

She nodded toward Gal Searcy, the dramatics counselor, who sat with her hands under her chin, her face
marked by make-up more defined than the others around
her were wearing. With the nod, it was as if Deree were
letting everyone know that she trusted Gal and knew
that not only the play but all of Festival Week would be
just as perfect as she expected it to be.

"When do you begin rehearsals for the play, Gal?"
she asked.

"Just before the White Water trip," Gal replied.

Ida, still eying the door, coughed into her hand and
coughed again, pulled her legs up under her, shifted
them like sticks, and then let a noise that was like the
squeak of an animated toy come from her tight mouth.
Deree paused as if in the hope of passing over the inter-
ruption without having to comment on it, and then
began again.

"The White Water ride is next week."

Bussi James, still wearing her clothes from the riding
ring, waved the paper she had taken from her pocket.

"I already have my girls." She spoke excitedly. "Ty
Barnet, Bobby Slater, Emmy Vann——"

Gee Gee dropped a hand hard on the speaker's arm.

"I was going to tell the girls myself." And then with
a stern eye: "Since Bussi's given them to you, we might
as well have them all. The others are Winnie Holt, Lissie Tate, Ruth Davis, and Esther Bellamy—I believe
that's the list."

lighted room, startled and somehow ashamed to find all of them sitting there as before—*fine, upstanding young women, symbols of perfect health of mind and body, the catalogue told you so.* They all appeared to be so exactly as they had been when she went out on the porch to find the figure on the ground that she felt she must be ill, or dreaming.

But they were beginning to move now, breaking up the meeting, going back to the cabins to check on the lights-out that came before taps were sounded on the slope by Mr. Mac. As Deree stood up, the cushion in her chair fell to the floor. Abby reached over and picked it up, speaking softly to the other in what she hoped was a voice she always used.

"Ida's gone down to check on Babs Todd." She kept her eyes fixed on Deree's.

Deree looked at her sharply, and then, reassured, offered that calm smile. With a gesture of affection that was rare for her, she took hold of Abby's arm and walked with her to the door. The two of them went together down the path along which Ida had managed to stumble a few minutes before.

"You're not very good at hiding your feelings," Deree said softly.

Abby's mouth went dry.

"I—I——" She was caught in the lie and did not know how to escape it.

"You wanted very much to go to White Water, didn't you?" The question was as soft as the night. "I could tell it by the look you had when the list was given us."

"I did want to go," Abby said. She had forgotten about the riding trip and now remembered it again.

"Well, you just haven't had enough horsemanship. But Bussi tells me you're doing well. So well you were almost chosen."

"I did want to go," Abby said again.

"I'm very pleased with you," Deree went on. "Gee Gee feels better, too, than she did. I'm going to tell your father so when I write him."

"You really needn't write him," Abby said, not knowing why the idea of the letter brought distress. "You can talk to him when he comes to see me."

"So he's coming."

"I don't know when. But it should be soon."

As they went along in the darkness, Deree stumbled over a root.

"I'm going to have to ask Mr. Mac to put a light here," she said crossly.

Taking her flashlight from her pocket, Abby threw a yellow pinpoint glow over the path that was taking them to Sky House, where the older girls were waiting for the song that meant good night. She turned the light toward a clump of laurel as if half-expecting to find a figure spread-eagled on the dark ground, and then turned it quickly away.

SIXTEEN

AFTER the camp and the lake had been left behind, the country had the wild, untrammeled look that
one still finds in the sparsely settled parts of the Appa-
lachian spine. It was as if no traveler had ever been here
before to place his mark on these mountains that were
as virgin as they had been before the first white man
came here, and even before that.

Over there that smoke signal sent up by phantom
Indians come back here to search for phantom buffalo
and wildcat. Over there a waterfall, down there ferns
in a ravine, and along that old track a tree half-fallen,
as if some giant creature had placed it there and then
gone away forgetful. This really might be a country
where no human had ever come, and, what was more,
where no human ever would come.

Even the station wagon that Mr. Mac drove toward
Flat Rock, his hands easy on the wheel, seemed to be an
anachronism as it moved over these wild shores of
ranges. A rifle, a sunbonnet, a skillet, belonged here. A
savage might appear from that cave and be less of a

surprise than the sign on the road that read: WHITE
WATER CLIFF. NO THOROUGHFARE FOR CARS.

As they moved to the tip of the ridge, the cliff itself
became apparent, rough in the sunlight and spearing
the sky in defiant glory. Not the tallest of the Smokies,
it still seemed to be more unapproachable than the
others, belonging in past time and in other worlds. White
Water Mountain stood lonely, dignified, lost, and silent,
so much by itself that anyone who looked at it might
feel, as Abby had felt in viewing the whole range, that
he was the only watcher who had ever come to this place.

"Nice cool day," Mr. Mac commented as they
rounded the last curve and the mountain was lost to
view. "But it's going to rain by noon."

"How do you know?"

"I can smell rain."

Like my father, she thought.

"Every day's nice in these mountains," she said.

He nodded.

"You ought to stick around and see this country in the
wintertime."

"Cold?"

"You bet. And lonesome."

"What do you do after camp closes?" she wanted to
know.

"In wintertime I hunt."

"My father got a lot of quail last year."

"Tell him to come up here for grouse with me." He twisted his corded neck. "You shoot?"

"Not very well." She did not tell him how much she hated the killing. "Last year I went deer driving with him."

"Did he get any game?"

"A fat old buck. He's very proud of it. I took a picture of him beside the deer. He'll show it to you on sight."

"I'd like to get a shot at one of the fellows myself."

"I hate to see them die."

He grinned.

"Shame to kill them pretty wild things." And with a look at his watch: "I bet that Flat Rock train is late again."

They were in the town now, with the mountains shut from their sight. The car went along a main street where on a Saturday morning men in jeans lounged to look at the tourists and spit and look away again. But today the place was quiet, with the shops on either side of the street almost empty, and with the café where the juke box blared a hot breath empty, too. Mr. Mac brought the car to a stop in front of the station at the far end of the street.

"You go in there and wait for Larry," he said. "I'll walk over to the Ridge Store and see about the lanterns."

She looked at him dubiously.

"How will I know Larry?"

"His friend Jake decided not to come this time." Mr. Mac chuckled. "Larry'll be the one who gets off the train."

Abby left him to go through the waiting room where the smell of disinfectant and urine had long ago become part of the atmosphere. As a clerk in an eyeshade that was like a disguise stared at her curiously she felt a sudden sense of dislocation at being away from the camp after the weeks shut up there. Outside, the boards of the platform were worn like the boards on the deck of a ship. She looked down the track where the train would come, and looked again, as if not sure it would arrive at all.

On a bench that dipped a little to the side she sat down to wait for the traveler. CHEW RITE TOBACCO FOR TENDER GUMS was the advice given on a sign beyond which a mule that did not need to be tied at all was held to a post by a strip of worn leather. In watching the mule and the red, jump-out color of the sign Abby felt almost giddy. But it was good to sit down in a place where the world was not dyed the color of the camp in the hills.

"Train from Saluda." The man in the eyeshade came from the ticket window to the platform, staring at her again as he bawled the words.

First came the shrill note of the whistle, and afterward the chugging of the still-invisible engine. From around a corner that was half-hidden by a jutting boulder the train appeared at last, coming in leaning sidewise. And Larry Stephens, what would he be like? Lisa's brother who was going to be a doctor as his father before him had been. As the daycoach pulled to a stop Abby went tentatively along the platform toward the box a porter put near the steps.

"Coach and freight." The eyeshade bobbled at her once again before it disappeared.

A tall fellow in a tweed coat came swinging down from the rear platform and began to walk toward Abby. His eyes had little red rims around them, and the collar of his shirt was dusty. When he spoke, his voice was too deep, as if he were trying to clear smoke out of it. But she liked him at once, or at least liked the way he looked. The traveler himself did not seem to like his looks at all.

"I'm Larry Stephens," he said. "Or what's left of him."

"I'm Abby Gregory," she replied.

"I've heard Mother speak of you." He blinked against the sun. "Are you the official greeting committee?"

"I'm not a very impressive one."

"I'm nothing for you to be meeting."

"Are you—ill?"

He smiled at her.

"That's one word for it."

"Have you been——" She hesitated.

"I have a hangover," he said. "My work's over for the summer so I celebrated."

"Is it bad?"

"Very." He looked at her in mock anxiety. "You won't tell on me at the camp, will you?"

"Of course not." ¯

"Emmy—she'll know, and that's all right." He looked at Abby more sharply. "Why didn't Emmy come with you?"

"Deree wanted her at camp." Abby hurried ahead. "Mr. Mac drove me. He's across the street at the Ridge Store."

"Let's get him."

They went across the street and into the store with its odors of grain, harness, and kerosene pinching their nostrils. Leaving Abby standing by the crate of lantern shades that were waiting by the door, Larry walked back with the men. At the counter, flanked by trout flies, Mr. Mac and the proprietor stood talking together. By next month the prospect for rainbow should be good, very good, yes, damn good. Mr. Mac turned and slapped Larry on the back.

"You got here," he said.

"On time, too."

"Rye?" the proprietor asked.

"Tempting fate again." Larry grinned. "Pour me a small one."

He downed the drink quickly, and turned away from the counter to come back to Abby. He looked a little dizzy now, shined up and ready to gallivant as her father would say, and somehow taller than before as he beckoned to her to come along. At the door she paused, eying Mr. Mac who was still at the counter by the trout flies. She wondered if Larry had forgotten him.

"Joe's coming over to camp this afternoon," Larry said. "He'll bring Mac and the lanterns."

As Abby walked beside Larry to the car she thought of her father's saying to her that nobody in his right mind would take a drink before ten o'clock in the morning. But Larry kept a straight enough line as they crossed the street and got into the car. In the car, as she sat very straight beside him, Larry glanced toward her as if realizing for the first time that she was a person and a girl.

"We're on our way," he said. "Cheers for Green Leaf."

She sat back, sniffing the fresh sweetness of the balsam, the pine, and the dampness a shower had brought. That after-the-rain odor was stronger than the odor of Lisa's brother beside her. He smelled of whisky, of shaving lotion, and a little cindery from the train. She noticed now the well-fitting clothes that hung easily on his body. No man she had ever known wore clothes quite that way, but she instinctively knew it was right.

He sat forward in the seat once again, seemingly unaware of her and of having any connection with her.

They rode in silence past a dipping slope where a farmer like a toy farmer plowed with a toy mule. Raindrops lingered like diamonds on the fir trees. Everywhere that odor of mist and mountains, one Abby would never be able to forget in the years to come, distinct in the air, rising over the smell of the exhaust pipe and the odor of shaving lotion.

"Do you approve of drinking?" Larry asked suddenly.

"I approve of my father. He smells like tobacco and rye."

"Mother despises it." He was talking more to himself than to Abby.

"She'd be angry if she knew you had one with the men?"

"More than angry," he replied soberly. "She knows what it can do——" He changed what he was beginning to say into something else. "She wouldn't tell you right out how she felt about it, and you wouldn't know until later." He shrugged bladelike shoulders. "Mother's a hard one to follow sometimes."

"'Follow that gleam right over the top of Old Stone Face,'" Abby said, imitating Emmy.

Larry threw back his head and laughed.

"Sometimes I think the truth is that Mother can't bear the thought of understanding herself," he said. "It would be like solving the riddle that keeps you going."

Abby spoke hesitantly.

"I never saw anybody like her."

"She's really something," he agreed. "Sometimes she gets all those ideas about pragmatic Christianity going around in her head the way this rye's going around in mine."

"How did she get so religious?"

He held the wheel more carefully.

"Before she married my father she wanted to make a career for herself in the church. Sometimes I think she still wants it. As Emmy says—follow that gleam right over the top of Old Stone Face. Only with Mother it has to be a very big mountain—like White Water."

"Some of the girls say, 'Follow the gleam to the latrine.'"

He was serious now in his laughter. Beside him, Abby looked down at her fingers, and then back at the road in front of her where White Water Mountain stood half-hidden by clouds. Deree really was in some kind of place like that. Or seemed to be. And Lisa, different and yet resembling her mother, also had her White Water, clothed in mists, but there and waiting to be climbed. Abby spoke to Larry.

"Lisa was talking to me about your father."

His words were guarded.

"What did she have to say about him?"

"That he was the finest man she had ever known."

He seemed suddenly about to stop the car, but instead sent it faster ahead, even though they were on a downgrade, with the lake road not far away now and the lower height of Old Stone Face hiding the highest ridge. He put his mind to the car, and to something beyond the car, before he at last gave Abby a reply.

"It's hard to tell what Lisa really thinks," he said. "Her mists are stronger than she is, although that isn't apparent to most people. Since Father died . . ."

He let the words die in his mouth as they turned off the highway into the private road that went along the lake's edge to the camp. When they came to the barred gate beyond which the buildings appeared, she saw that his face was whiter than it had been when they left the Ridge Store and started over the mountain for Green Leaf. But at the parking lot, when he spoke to her, it was with a simulated gayety.

"Here we are in Mother's Paradise!"

In front of Tip Top House, as he pulled his baggage from the station wagon, they could see, through the trees, the shapes of the campers in the cove where assembly was held on a fine morning such as this one had started out to be before the clouds began coming over the mountains. Now, with the assembly half over, the girls were singing, with the words of the hymn coming up the slope toward Larry and Abby.

> *"Dear Lord and Father of mankind,*
> *Forgive our feverish ways,*
> *Reclothe us in our rightful mind*
> *In purer lives our service find,*
> *In deeper reverence praise. . . ."*

Larry pulled a jacket from the car. He looked up the slope toward the cabin that was reserved for his visit before he looked at Abby again.

"I've been talking too much," he said. "That drink in Flat Rock."

"Nobody will know."

"That's good." He straightened his shoulders. "I'll clean up and then come down to find Mother." As he walked away he spoke again. "See you in church, Abby."

SEVENTEEN

THE spiritual landscape of the camp was intensified on mornings like this one, at the assembly hour. Deree led the assembly standing before a cairn of stones with the girls in a circle before her. The dell with its just-cut grass had a smell like fresh hay, and the girls with their fresh young faces were like flowers. Behind them lay the slope of the mountain and the spread of the lake.

Above them the clouds moved against each other and then moved apart. For a moment it would seem as if a deluge might be on its way over the mountain, and in the next moment a patch of blue sky would appear.

Cloudy weather, changing weather, and more threatening than it had been a little while ago, as Abby joined the others for assembly after leaving Larry on the hill.

Near the edge of the crowd she sat down, watching Deree. Larry's words came back to her as she sat with the others, the suddenly appearing sun soaking into her. *See you in church.* The words were too true. This secluded spot, with the girls guardedly intent, watching every movement Deree made, was like some hidden cathedral with the world shut away beyond boundaries that had lost their power.

"Did Larry come?" Emmy whispered slyly as she inched toward Abby past an intervening camper.

"He's here."

"Ugly of Deree, not letting me go with you." Then softly, "Did he ask for me?"

"First thing."

As Emmy relaxed with a delighted sigh, Abby glanced across an open space where a group of counselors were sitting together on a slope. Peg sat among the others, her face attentive, but Abby knew that she was probably thinking about the love Freddie wrote down in the letters that came every day. As if caught spying on Peg, Abby turned her eyes toward Ida, the riding counselor, who sat by herself at the end of the row.

The face with its stretched skin wore an attitude of attention that at first glance might delude a watcher into thinking this one a replica of the other faces in the dell. But behind the mask, waiting to assert itself, was the face Abby had seen on the ground that night at Fir Lodge when Deree had sent her on an errand and had been brought back a lie. Moving backward toward that night, Abby swallowed uneasily.

She stared at Deree, who was wearing a look that was as clear as the little patch of sky where no clouds moved. Abby's own eyes were tight with the thought of Deree's words to be. But even in the moment of assuming the role of a supplicant, she found herself wishing passionately to be able to feel the amused acceptance that had come for a moment into Larry's eyes as he left her a little while ago.

"I want to remind you once again," Deree began. Then she spoke.

> "First day I came—magnificent
> The morning rose in memorable pomp,
> Glorious as e'er I had beheld. In front
> The lake lay laughing. Just a footstep near
> The solid mountain shone, bright as the cloud,
> Grain tinctured, drenched in empyrean light.
> And in the meadows and the lower ground,
> Was all the sweetness of the common dawn—
> Dew-vapors and the melody of birds
> And laborers going forth to till the fields.
> Ah—need I say, dear friend, that to the brim,
> My heart was full: I made no vows, but vows
> Were then made for me; bond unknown to me
> Was given, that I should be, else sinning greatly,
> A dedicated spirit . . ."

Her wide-open eyes turned from the girls to the sky and back to the campers again. Abby, wishing still for acceptance, felt a deep anger, as if the words were a sham and she herself being made into an unwilling slave to them. But they must be true or Deree would not repeat them for all to hear. And you ought to believe in them. The inability to believe as strongly as Deree did brought a deep shame, exiling her from this Eden in which the others, except Ida, sat so comfortably.

"I want to talk to you this morning about the love of God," Deree said.

Lovely in her framework of leaves and stone, she stood quiet, her eyes, which were like cold gentians, catching and holding the eyes of the campers. Hers was a power frightening in its depth. Not a doubt that as she stood there she was able to send out some hidden self, and to draw her watchers into that self. But whatever the power, it would never be caged or even caught for a moment by some flicking hand.

"Do you hear that bird?" she asked suddenly.

From the hillside came a long, high trill, swelling into the silence that lay over the slope where the devotees sat watching and listening. It was only a bird's call, and yet with it, or at least so it seemed to Abby, came a moment so ecstatic that it was hard to come back down to the ground. The lark had seemed to split its heart and then relapse into nothingness as if by command from

that higher power Deree believed directed her relationship with all living things.

"I think of each of you as a bird," she went on. "God
is the father bird Who covers you with His wings. In
Him shall you trust."

Again Abby became unwillingly aware of Ida's face
against the background of leaves. The face was drawn
like the visage of a saint on the rack, tortured from trying to appear similar to the other faces and knowing it
could never be done. Abby looked at Ty Barnet who
was lifting an oily big paw to a cheek that was greasy
with the lard of sanctity. Abby's own eyes became black
with anger as she brought her glance back to Deree.

"In God's love we can all be filled with 'such delight
as prisoned birds must find in freedom.' We can wing
our way over the dark fields of fear to the pastures of
love."

Abby's hands were clenched hard together. Sometimes, even while trying to believe in God, you just
could not keep from being afraid, and Deree ought not
to stand here before everybody and say you could. She
had known since her mother's death that it never happened that way and that there was no use in thinking it
ever would. And yet, maybe in some way Deree was
right, after all—surely you could not make up a thing
like that—evidently she did have some kind of secret
bond with a Father of her own.

"Sometimes the earth around you will be parched, and the sun will blister you. But God's grace will lead you again to still waters."

From the corner of her eye Abby glimpsed the lake that was lying too still under clouds that had begun to rush through the troubled sky above Old Stone Face. In her place beside Emmy she moved restlessly. A parched dryness in her throat made her suddenly wish for a drink to gulp down as Larry had gulped his this morning in Flat Rock. Embarrassed by such a desire at such a time, she touched her tongue with her finger and then slid her hand into her pocket, feeling doubly shameful because she wanted to guffaw at her own gesture.

"Your deepest obligation lies within you—in keeping yourself close to God. Then peace will come to you."

She spoke the words the campers had heard her speak often before.

> "If I have faltered more or less
> In my great task of happiness,
> If I have moved among my race,
> And shown no glorious morning face,
> If beams from happy human eyes
> Have moved me not; if morning skies,
> Books, and my food, and summer rain
> Knocked on my sullen heart in vain:
> Lord, thy most poignant pleasure take
> And stab my spirit broad awake."

She's right, Abby thought. All of them were right. Every single person sitting here on this slope. Even Ty Barnet with that bacon grease of sanctity. The wrong lay in being different from the others, in not being able to make the bargain, or even to believe in the bargain that would bring you home safe in the end. You take care of God and He'll take care of you. Not gambling, the way her father did at the club, but a fair exchange that people like Deree knew how to make.

The wrong was not in Deree or in God but in herself. She stared at Deree with the shame open in her face.

EIGHTEEN

Lisa came to the assembly late, sitting down with the counselors on the little sloping rise to the left of the cairn of stones. Her face had a look very like Deree's, and yet was peculiarly Lisa's own. Larry had been entirely wrong this morning when he spoke of mists. Not a suggestion of doubt anywhere in her face. Instead, a certainty that was stamped into the visage, not to be taken away. She has something I've wanted and sought, hunted and failed to find, since I can remember, Abby thought, still watching.

And yet, in another way, this person was not a person at all. Those pink flowerlike cheeks, the rounded body, the graceful hands were only the outer veil of an impersonal loveliness. Lisa represented the desires that never seemed to have had a home. This was the immortal hand and eye but framed for a destiny not fearful. Here were the stars that throw down their spears and water heaven with tears of hope. Here was the impossible beauty, so close and yet never to be caught.

"And now," Deree was saying in one of her characteristically quick moves from the pastures of purity into fields that might have been clipped by a lawn mower. "Gee Gee wants a moment to talk with you about the ride to White Water."

It seemed to Abby that as the tall counselor strode forward the girls, as usual, stopped being themselves and became soldiers with the board backs and flat bodies of recruits. Rank and file were readying themselves to follow over hill, over dale, right up the cliff of White Water into the sky, if that were demanded of them. She could see platoons of campers exploding through the clouds that were coming faster now, sliding over the mountain and darkening the lake.

"As all of you know by now," Gee Gee began, "the White Water ride is a high point in our Green Leaf season."

Tall and erect before the girls on the grass, she was, in spite of her stiff posture and high cheekbones, somehow like Deree, after all. They were so close in their beliefs that they had become alike in knowing how to take it for granted that anything they demanded of the Green Leaf campers was the best and only the best in the best of all possible worlds. But surely that was right. If you were the captain, as Deree had called Gee Gee that day in Cape Fear, then you had to be certain, not only for yourself, but for the others under your command.

But suppose your commands, given with such authority, were in error, after all? Or suppose—and this was worse—that you as the person in charge had to give orders that would sacrifice the one for the many. And then there was always the person who could not obey you, even when you gave him a chance. To see him being half left behind because he could not help it must be the worst thing you had to watch.

"I want to talk first about the camp play." Gee Gee checked it in the notebook she held in her hand. "*Midsummer-Night's Dream*—a good play for Green Leaf."

"Do you have the cast?" Deree asked gently.

"Gal is posting the names of the players this morning. They'll be on the bulletin board by noon." She cleared her throat. "Now I'll give you news of the riding trip."

"When do we go?" Ty called.

"We'll post the time by noon," Gee Gee replied. "And one more thing. I want to remind all of you again that the trip is only a prelude to the Fire Night Ceremony when we give our honors to our girls. Being chosen for those honors is the most significant event that can happen to you."

"How many will be chosen this year?" Peg asked.

"We'll keep it at eight." Gee Gee gave the watching campers a smile that was like cold, invigorating water. "The best eight in the camp."

"All new?"

"We never repeat honors. We began the policy the year Lisa was our first honor girl." She gave Lisa a dash of her cold smile. "But we do ask Lisa to help with the Fire Night Ceremony."

Abby saw the eight faces near the big fire in the dell, and each face was her own. Flames from the great ceremonial fire spiraled higher in her mind, obscuring the mists that had begun to slide in from the lake. Here was Fire Night with Deree and Gee Gee like twin priestesses, and with Abby Gregory stepping forward, her head in a halo. Abby Gregory, first at White Water, first for Deree, first in the heart of Gee Gee Stern. But in the caricature lay a grotesque spark of hope.

"If there's nothing else, we'll have the parting song." Gee Gee turned away, showing a smart pair of heels to the crowd of campers.

"For the beauty of the earth,
For the beauty of the skies,
For the love which from our birth,

Over and around us lies,
Lord of all to Thee we raise,
This our hymn of grateful praise."

The voices took the words to the sky, pouring them out as a little while ago the bird in the forest had poured out his sweet, shrill song. Ida, the mask-faced counselor, sang with the others, but Abby did not sing. Instead, she watched the rain, very close now in a moving curtain, and on them all at once, sending the crowd scuttling over the damp grass toward the porch of Sky House. She ran hard up the steps and almost into the arms of Larry Stephens.

"A bad break," he said. "Sudden squall—that sometimes happens to sweetness and light."

NINETEEN

THE heat of the day, scathing for these heights, beat down on the dahlias in the Green Leaf garden and projected itself through the window into the Craft Shop with its Navajo rugs, red, white, and gold, and its shelves of pottery so bright that they seemed to pick up the exotic color of the dahlias outside. Everywhere the hot sunlight, stabbing at Abby's eyes as she bent over the rug of fire-engine red—the color dear to Henry's heart—that she was still making to take back with her to Cape Fear when the summer was over.

"It's going very slowly, isn't it?" Peg said, leaving her desk to come over for a look at the pattern of the rug.

Abby shook her head.

"I'll never get done with it. Not even by Festival Week." She pushed the rug away. "Another letter from Jim Brandon came this morning. He's going to Furlong to start football practice just about the time camp closes."

"You'll miss him in Cape Fear?" Peg asked.

"He may come by here to see me on Visitors' Day."

Peg looked at her searchingly.

"You don't seem exactly wild to see him, Abby."

Abby picked up her rug again. "The dates may not be right," she said, threading a red strand through her fingers. "Have you made up your mind yet about staying over after camp?"

Peg looked dubious.

"Deree still wants me to help with closing up the crafts," she replied. "But Freddie just won't put up with it."

Abby twisted the thread again.

"Lisa spoke to me about staying over with her for a few days."

"Abby," Peg began, more dubious than before, "it

really isn't my affair, but if I were you I wouldn't linger here with Lisa after the season."

"Why not?"

"I—I think that by the time camp's over you'll be ready to go home."

"But I'd like to be here with Lisa."

"Well—let's put it this way then." Peg sat down beside her. "Lisa may be ready for you to go."

Abby spoke quickly.

"You've no right to say a thing like that."

Peg stood up again. "Keep shop for me, will you? I want to run down to the Lodge."

As the counselor moved away, Abby bent over the rug, then restlessly stood up, leaving her unfinished work on the window seat. Through the window she stared at the garden where the dahlias on the hill, now in midsummer, were heavy on the stalks, some of them breaking under their own weight. At the near row stood Mr. Mac, snippers in hand, cutting the bouquet he arranged each day for the dining room. To the left of him, on the clay road, stood the covered wagon he was driving to White Water next week for the riding trip.

"You still at that rug?" someone asked.

Abby turned to find Emmy beside her making a quince face.

"I've got to finish it," she replied. "If only to show I can."

"If that were the reason with me, I'd never get to the

end of anything," Emmy said. "To get on with it at all, I have to want to do something."

Abby looked through the window at the covered wagon near the garden.

"You want to go to White Water, don't you?" she asked.

"In a halfhearted way. But I'm not going."

"Not going?"

"Larry thinks he may be coming back to camp that weekend."

"I didn't even know he'd gone away."

"He went over last night to see Jake Dean at Cray Lake. But he may come back, and if he does, I intend to be here."

Abby looked at her soberly.

"How are you going to get out of going on the trip?"

"I'm already out." She giggled. "I got Gal to tell Deree that she simply had to have me to help her direct the play."

Abby picked up the rug again, not working on it, just holding it in her lap. Understanding how a person really manages to get what he wants and how he can get done what he wants to do did not get any easier as time went along. Here was Emmy, she told herself, telling a lie to stay home from a trip I've been dying to be chosen for. A shadow of comfort came in the remembrance that she might have the curse the day of the ride or soon after. I'd go, anyway, she decided, if they'd have me.

"Where's Peg?" Emmy asked with a belated glance around the shop.

"Down at the Lodge."

Emmy stood up, looking at herself in the mirror above the desk, yawning as she spoke.

"Well, I've got to get myself ready to shoot an arrow into the air."

"If it's like the rest of yours, it'll probably fall to earth before it leaves the bow."

"Exactly," Emmy said. She stared at Abby with sudden open curiosity. "What did your letter say?"

"How did you know I had one?"

"I peeked in the box."

"Jim—" she bent her head—"Jim may hitchhike up here to see me. On his way to football practice at Furlong."

"I want to meet this Jim," Emmy teased. "Either here or in Cape Fear when I visit you there."

"Then you really are coming to visit me?"

"I've already written Aunt Anson my plans." She winked before turning to go through the door. "Maybe I'll be stealing your boy friend."

When Emmy had gone, Abby looked at her rug and then glanced through the window again at the garden where Mr. Mac came back down the slope, knelt by the

wagon to test a shaft, and then went back to his flowers. With a quick move he snipped one last blossom,
hawked loudly, and spit a brown tobacco stain into the
earth. When he paused again to restake a plant that had
dropped toward the earth, Abby started to call him, but
at the sound of Lisa's voice she turned sharply.

"No customers?" Lisa asked, giving the shop a skep-
tical glance.

"Not unless you're one," Abby said.

"I was sent to take over."

"Where's Peg?"

"She's helping Gal decide on my costume for the
play."

Lisa stepped closer. "I was teasing you about taking
over," she said. "Peg will be back any moment."

Abby kept looking at her.

"I didn't know you were in the play."

"I'm Titania."

She really could be, Abby thought.

"You didn't read for a part?" Lisa asked.

"I don't know anything about acting."

"You could learn."

Abby still stared at her.

"Where did you learn?"

"Oh, I've acted in the summers here. And in New
York, I learned a lot about it going to the theater with
my father."

Abby looked out of the window at the spare figure

that had left the garden and was moving up the hill, his arms full of flowers.

"What are you staring at?" Lisa wanted to know.

"Mr. Mac." Abby turned from the window. "He makes me think of *my* father."

Lisa took a seat on the window ledge.

"You never talk much about your father," she said. "Don't you like him?"

"Oh, very much."

"You funny child."

"My father's not very much like the people you know," Abby said defensively. "But you'll see for yourself when he comes to the camp."

Patting the window ledge in invitation for Abby to sit next to her, Lisa offered an arch glance.

"You'd better hope he doesn't come next weekend," she said.

"Why not?"

The smile was a dazzle.

"It's the White Water ride, and you're going."

When Abby spoke it was as if the words had been pushed twice into her throat before they managed to get back out into the air.

"So I'm going, after all."

"You were chosen in Emmy's place—Gal wants her for the play. Lucky you. A good chance for honors."

Abby spoke flatly.

"You're sure I'm going?"

"They posted your horse."

"Gineral?"

"Yes."

As Lisa moved closer along the window ledge, Abby had once more the sense of being pushed. It came so strongly that suddenly, for no reason at all except maybe the heat, the room began to slide at an angle. Holding the rug too tightly, she bent forward, losing her grip on it, letting it slide to the floor. As she reached down to pick it up, Lisa's hand closed over the circle of her wrist, and Abby began to stare at the ring which was by now familiar but somehow more fascinating than ever before.

"So you like the ring." Lisa laughed softly.

"I—I do. Very much."

"Would you want a ring of your own?"

"I hadn't ever thought of it," Abby said. It seemed to her that the heat was more insistent, stabbing at her through the window, dark red like the dahlias on the slope of the hill.

"Would you?"

"I don't know." She pulled her hand away. "Oh, Lisa, I'm all mixed up."

"You don't have to be, you know."

As they sat there the sun heat outside sent little waves of air curlicueing up from the dahlias toward a hot blue bowl of sky. The sight of the ring on the hand lying now over her own brought Abby a great confusion and a beating of the heart so hard that it must be a dream beat. Then the hand went away, and with it the confusion began to go. What was the matter with her anyway?

As Peg came up the path and through the door, Lisa dressed her words in the organdy of her laughter.

"It's marvelous, your going to White Water," she said. "I know you can't wait for the trip!"

TWENTY

THIS was a country of dreams and of heights, with every now and then a boulder in the path as a barrier, so that the horses had to pick their way around it and find the trail again. Here laurel, there rhododendron, and always the ache inside of her, worse than she had believed it could be by the time they came to the high mountain spring and dismounted for a rest before going the last small distance to the camp on the White Water cliffside.

It had begun to get worse this morning when they left the camp, following the wagon trail with the sun just up and with Mr. Mac two hours ahead of them. For a while the pain had been better, but now the ache inside of her made Abby feel as if she was riding a merry-go-round and going in circles around the sawdust ground of some dream Fair instead of moving along the mountain path on the broad back of Gineral.

As the riders went through the fern-damp forest to the cleared spot at the spring, she bent forward to pat her mount, feeling that to give in to her sense of illness was to be a traitor not only to herself but to the animal that had carried her so gently along the trail during the hours since they had left the camp this morning. Among scrubby bushes she dismounted, trying not to wince at the pain of the movement.

"A drink will sure taste good," Ty called from across the way.

"Sure will."

Abby went to the spring and bathed her face with the cool water. She went back to Gineral, patting him with a damp hand, hating the sense of being unable to see him clearly. But maybe it would go. And there was only a little journey left to the camp site. Half an hour—even less than that, and she would have made it at last to the top of the cliff.

"Pat your face with this." Bobby Slater handed her a damp handkerchief. "It feels wonderful."

She stood there staring at Bobby, hating the pink cheeks and the clear eyes that stared back at her. With a too-quick gesture she handed the other the cloth and swung herself into the saddle. Now the landscape merged into a hazy mass, with the laurel and the ferns running together and with the path a vague clearing that lay stretched into forever in front of Gineral's nose. But they were almost there.

"Let's go," Bussi shouted.

At the command, they went forward for the last little distance, with Abby in the line behind Bussi, keeping her eyes on the counselor's broad back. You did not give up just because you felt bad, she told herself. Not when it was your own fault for coming. You took it and were quiet about it. But what you really wanted was to call out to Gee Gee. May I speak to you, Miss Stern? May I have a word with you, Miss Stern? I wanted to come on the trip so I came anyway—but now I've got to go home. She bent with the ache as they reached a long curve that led to the plateau near the cliff where camp would be made.

"This is it," Bussi yelled. "Got here in good shape!"

"And Mac beat us in."

Gee Gee's laugh was like a light bark in the thin air of the mountains. The riders dismounted, handling the reins gently, loosening the girths from the sweaty horses. Near the camp site was a closed-in pasture, and close to it stood the wagon like a house to protect the campers if rain came. Close by was the log pile Mr. Mac had prepared for the fire which would keep out the cold of the nearing night.

Night would bring fire and stars and rest, Abby told

herself, staring at the logs. With an effort she turned away to take Gineral to the pasture and loose him there now that she had rubbed him down. Night would bring fire and stars and rest and sleep. Then she would lie under her blanket, not cold as she was now, and not dizzy with the imagined words to Gee Gee beginning to slither in her head again as she came near the fire.

I shouldn't have come, Miss Stern, but maybe you know how it is. I've been wanting to come, and Lisa thought I should come when the chance came. She told me this was one of the things I'd been living for since that April morning back home in the low country. Nothing but pines there, and foamy fields warm to lie down in. A warm wind there—and rain is in the west wind—not cold like the wind that comes off the face of the mountain, cutting around corners and coming fast at the camp.

As the thoughts slithered faster than before in her head, the campers came to the fire one by one, Ellie with the jodphurs that had never fit and Bobby whose brown cool eyes always looked as if they were seeing past you into eyes more important than your own. Then Ceci, the assistant who had come on the trip in place of Ida, who was ill again and unable to ride.

"A song," Ty called.

> *"A keeper would a-hunting go,*
> *And over his shoulder he carried a bow,*

All for to shoot a merry little doe,
Among the leaves so green.

Jackie Boy?
Master.
Sing you well?
Very well!
Hey down. Ho down.
Derry Derry down.
Among the leaves so green."

Very well indeed, Abby thought, looking at the sky where a white moon swam overhead. Merry little doe and I'm one the keeper didn't miss. She walked to the patch of ground where the riders had begun to move briskly under Gee Gee's orders, arranging blankets and preparing the supper that would soon be ready. Even standing close to the fire, Abby trembled. I'm colder than I've been since the day my mother died, she thought, spreading out her blanket roll with fingers that were blue at the tips.

"That's a good space you chose," Bussi said. "Put your poncho over the blanket. We're going to have a cold night."

A cold night, Abby thought. A cold space, this one near the cliff. A space with no leaves, no shelter, and with the wagon which had seemed so solid a skeleton shape in the violet dusk. She took a deep, forced breath of icy air that went clean through her body and down into her belly. At the fire she spread her hands, watching the girls fill the tin plates with the food they were serving for supper. It has to be eaten, she thought. Somehow it has to be eaten.

"Bacon and beans," Bussi called.

The fire was higher now, jumping to the sky with the flames gulping at a cold darkness that had fallen suddenly out of nowhere. The odors of grease, fat, and the black smell of boiling coffee in a tin pot chewed at her insides. When Ty handed her a plate she sat watching the beans and bacon with a profound distaste. After a moment she moved away from the half circle of girls near the fire and went to the wagon which had stopped being a skeleton and had become a masked shape in the half-light of the rising moon.

"Abby." She whirled at Bussi's call.

"I thought maybe you were taking a look at the horses."

"I wanted to be by myself."

The counselor's eyes were curious.

"Is something wrong with you?"

"No, no. Nothing."

Ty called out from her place in the circle of riders near the fire.

"Bussi, when did the first Green Leaf trip come to White Water?"

"Ten years ago."

This one might have been going on that long, Abby thought.

"It was cold then, too," Bussi was saying. "But in the morning, when we waked up, the view from the cliff was magnificent."

Abby had to get away. The group by the fire was one thing and she was false and wrong to it. She went past the wagon, a dark hulk edged in silver, wanting to hide her face in its black depths and never show it again. Uncertainly she went down the path to the cliff's face. At the ledge many images came rushing through her mind like wings, like birds that had flown from the valley over the rolling country and into the cold night of her mind.

She wiped her forehead, trying to brush the wings away, frightened because they resembled the old fears of home and more frightening because they had come to her so strongly in this strange place. I'm strange myself, she thought. And will be stranger unless I brush away these wings that are tearing me to pieces on the top of this mountain and that are tearing up the mountain, too.

As in a mist she began to see Lisa's face hanging in the air and to hear dark, terrible words falling from that proud mouth, with ice in every word. Summer, which had started with the doe, was by paradox a cold time— a time when you had lost your loneliness, or thought you did, only to have it come again colder in the moonlight. It made one ache. It made wind whistle through one.

She stepped right to the ledge, looking over still valleys with the moonlight falling over them, shimmering in the deep place, lighting mothlike in the crevasses, all shimmering, all asleep, all beautiful. And I am not beautiful, Abby thought. I want to get out of the dark, out of the moonlight. I want not to be lonesome like the still valley lying down there in the cold nighttime.

At the edge now, the very edge, before the hollows, before the deep spaces that were cutting away from the edge of the mountain as if a sword had cut the earth apart, the dream died, the illusions dried up, the terrible hopes became more terrible. In the dark she heard a long breath without knowing it was her own. She ran too quickly back to the others to sit down among them like a dead person killed by the long ride back from the depths, to sit with the girls by the fire but not of them.

"A song again," Lissie said.

Nobody seemed to have missed her, not one of the girls in the group by the fire that had a bright red warmth. Not even Bussi, gone now to the far side of the wagon to talk with Gee Gee in whispers that carried thinly toward the girls, seemed aware of her at all. This, for the riders, was the time before sleeping, the most intimate of all the hours. With the flames lighting the faces of the girls, faces easy in the interval between journeying and sleeping, this was a world that for these travelers was what it should be.

> *"On a Chinese honeymoon,*
> *In the merry month of June,*
> *Together we will wander,*

Where the cherry blossoms bloom.
We'll buy a toy balloon,
And sail up to the moon;
Together we will wander . . ."

Lissie, young, brown, with cheeks stained a near-cherry red, and with a guitar in her hand, led the gauzy song in a husky contralto that gave the words more depth than they would ever naturally possess. Her face, like all the faces in the circle, held the light of longing and the shadow of nebulous desires that were still unformulated, still waiting to be born. By the fire, their shoulders touching, the girls had a loveliness and gentleness. If I'm one of them, Abby thought, I'm the one with a sword that is going to fall right out of the sky on me.

"Abby."

At the rasp of Gee Gee's command she went to the wagon near the corral.

"Are you ill?"

"I'm all right."

The black, snake-whip eyes were on her.

"You're blue as skim milk."

"I'm cold."

"All summer you've been training for this ride to the cliff. And now you're cold." She eyed Abby shrewdly. "What is really the matter?"

Abby pulled Jim's sweater closer around her throat but it brought no warmth. She stood facing Gee Gee, but staring past her at the cliff where the moon was swimming in the sky, with the abyss lying far below like some white sea with tremendous waves, very still in the night, each one caught in its place. This was a place farther than she had ever expected to come, and had she known of the abyss, she would never have tried to come at all.

"Are you ill?" And with a sharper light in her eyes. "You knew before we left camp that you were going to be sick. Didn't you? That this was the time for it. You knew and didn't tell."

"I didn't tell you."

Abby turned away from her and went back to the circle of campers near the fire. Her mind was clear now, with the terror of a little while ago swept away. Huddled in her sweater, she sat with the others. It was not the curse that made her feel as she did. Not just that. She was in deep, in strangely, and did not know how to get out. She could turn, twist, try to double back, but nothing was going to do any good. The real illness lay in her knowledge of that.

"Roll that log on the fire, Abby," Bobby called.

Dragging the log toward the fireplace where the wood lay crisscross under the flames, she bent forward and fell flat on her face.

TWENTY-ONE

THE Infirmary, a log house like the others, was built on a slope removed from the center of the camp. Set apart in a grove of trees, it had an intervening space beyond them to muff into silence the talk of campers lounging on porches and in cabins. The building was divided into two sections, each a unit in itself, separate from the others. The rear room, to which Abby had been assigned, was open to the morning sun.

Like the Craft Shop, the Infirmary was nearer to the camp flower garden than it was to the lake and to Sky House. This window gave a view of the dahlia bed, and beyond it in a field goldenrod, just opening, with the green buds tight on stems that were swaying in a wind that came down the face of the mountain and up the slope.

From the cot she would be leaving before the day was over, Abby watched the sunlight stream past the trees on the hill to touch the dahlias in the field beyond. The leaves of the trees were so thin in the sunlight that it almost seemed as if you could stare through them to the cove on the far side of Sky House.

In the time of being alone in this room, and of traveling back in her mind over the days since she came to the camp, Abby had lost much of the sense of desolation that had been so strong at the cliffside. That time by the white valley had taken on the quality of a nightmare that is far enough behind so that you wonder if you dreamed it at all. In this gentle sunlight fear was lulled into a morning sleep.

As she lay there the voices came from the door, with Mr. Mac saying, "You'll find her in the room back there." And in reply the deep, rumbling tones that could belong only to her father. Sitting very straight on the cot, she stared unbelievingly at his figure as he came through the door. Then, conscious of the cigar and of the dark eyes behind it, she knew that he had really come to her.

As he bent over to kiss her she put her arms around his neck and held him close. He wore his blue serge coat, rough against her face. As he moved away from the bed to sit down in the chair across from her she saw that his trousers needed pressing. But he had a daisy in his buttonhole. And with him he had brought into the room the faint odor that was like the fields at home.

"I thought I'd surprise you," he said. "Instead, you've surprised me. Thought I'd find you gallivanting."

"I'm getting out of here this afternoon," she said.

"Sure you're all right?"

"I'm sure."

When he touched the flower in his buttonhole, giving it the same care he gave his flowers at home, she had a fierce moment of wondering why she had ever left him to come here. And in the same moment, as she looked again at his burned skin and sharp eyes, it began to seem to her that she had really never left him, and that the world of the camp did not exist at all.

"I came by on my way over to Pisgah instead of waiting until after I picked up my plants," he said. "That fellow Mac tells me I missed your Mrs. Stephens."

"Missed her?"

"She and some other woman went over to Flat Rock this morning." He bent toward her again. "Nice fellow, that Mac. I showed him the picture you took of me and my buck."

Abby grinned at him.

"He asked you to come back to shoot grouse, didn't he?"

"He asked me, and he wants me to send him some sea oats." He chewed at the cigar. "We'll go down to the beach and cut a load of oats for him just as soon as you get home. I'll have plenty of time. The asters will be finished. And the mums won't be ready for shipping until fall."

"How do your mums look?"

"With any luck I'll be cutting them by the middle of September."

The fields with their long rows of yellow, white, lavender, with the pungent foliage beneath the blossoms, seemed suddenly everywhere. Looking through the window, Abby felt a need for home that was deeper than any she had ever known. I was a fool, she told herself, ever to leave those fields. She looked at her father and saw him smiling at her.

"I got news for you," he said.

"What is it?"

"Didn't Miss Matthis write to you?"

"No. Tell me."

"They gave you the scholarship to Steeple Hill," he said. "The one you talked to the professor about."

Abby traveled back to the spring, to her own uncertainty under the eyes of the professor who had come down from the university to talk to the students in the high school. The scholarship had seemed as far away as White Water, and now it belonged to her. Now it was her own. Perhaps it would be like that with learning to belong to Green Leaf. Only afterward would she know her place for what it was. Only afterward, when the summer was behind.

"What's the matter with you?" her father said. "Aren't you pleased about the scholarship?"

She spoke at last.

"I'm proud that they gave it to me."

"I went by and thanked Miss Matthis when she gave me the news," he said. "You go see her yourself the day you get home."

"It won't be long now," Abby said, "until I'm back at the farm with the rest of you."

"You'll get there and go again," he reminded her. "When I left, Janie was talking about finishing your college clothes as soon as she got done with Henry's pants." He bent forward, taking his big old-fashioned watch from his pocket. "Well, I got to be moving if I'm going to pick up those plants."

"You just got here."

"I really do have to get along, Abby."

"What's so important about the plants?"

"They're for Miss Anson Vann."

"They'll keep."

"She won't."

Abby spoke slowly.

"Have you seen Jim?"

Her father stood up, staring down at her.

"He misses you. We all miss you, Abby." And then brusquely, "Well, I'd better pick up my passenger."

"Passenger?"

"Mr. Mac asked me to give a lift to some woman who's sick. She's been in the room over there"—he jerked his thumb toward the door—"across from yours. Take her as far as Boone so that she can get the train there tonight."

Abby sat up.

"Who is it?"

"I don't know. Some woman who had a fit on the floor in front of a crowd of kids. Not a very good thing, I'd say."

"Is—is she all right?"

"They're sending her home today. Don't want her around here."

Abby sat there staring past him at the wall. *Don't tell —don't tell. They'll send me home.* The foam on the lips, the jerking limbs, the staring faces of the campers, and Deree's face, calm as the morning. It would not be hard for Deree to get her away. Just tell her to go home and then spend the morning in Flat Rock so you didn't have to watch it. It doesn't matter who gets hurt, just so it is not Green Leaf. Abby lay against the pillow, wanting to shut out remembrance of Ida's face as it had been that night at Fir Lodge.

"Take care of yourself, Abby," her father said.

He kissed her quickly and went through the door with no other good-by. Watching the empty space where he had stood, she knew the loneliness that comes of being shut out of one world and of no entry into a new one. Suddenly, staring through the open door at the room across the way, where Ida must have been all the time, she put her head down and wept.

When she looked up it was to see Lisa, so fresh that it was as if she brought the morning in with her. For a moment Lisa stood watching, and then, as Abby sat up, she came to the bed, and pushed the cover away, smoothing the pillow with the white hand circled in the gold that held the sapphire.

"Why, you're crying."

"It's nothing."

"I came up to see you, and to tell Ida good-by, but she's gone."

"Deree shouldn't have sent her away," Abby said.

"She's ill. Going home is the best thing for her." Lisa looked from the bed to the window. "Mac told me your father was here."

"He gave Ida a lift in to Boone." Abby heard the same words coming again. "Deree shouldn't have sent her away."

"I think that's Mother's own affair," Lisa said gently. And closer now, very close: "You miss your mother, don't you?"

"Sometimes I do."

"I know." As she spoke the room seemed to glow with a light that spread everywhere. "The girls in my cabin are going to the Dell to spend Saturday night. Come over to see me then. I have something for you, Abby. And must talk to you alone."

TWENTY-TWO

As THE bugler sounded taps, the girls in the cabins lay listening to the notes that were pulled out into the darkness like taffy. In the moment the bugle sounded, the noises of lake and hillside went to nothing. It was as if the go-to-sleep music were the only sound in the world. The silent girls on the cots seemed bound to listen, made to listen and lie still as dying till the notes fell in clusters into the night.

From her cot, arms under her head, Abby glanced at the rafters which hung like crossbars in the light of the waning moon. Lifting herself on an elbow, she stared at Peg's vacant cot and then lay back against her pillow. This was usually a good time, a quiet one when you got into your own bed and lay in silence until your thoughts were drowned in the lake of sleep. This was the hour like the one at home when you went back in dream to meet your gone self and the gone mother you wanted to meet. But tonight was different.

She thought of Lisa and of how quickly she had become close to her. One day a ring began to close around you, and you did not know it was there at all. One day you saw the water lilies and remembered the doe. One day you were riding back to camp with a Larry who talked to you—*I've talked too much,* he'd said—about his mother and about Lisa. One day you were laughing in the Craft Shop with Emmy who was coming to Cape Fear with you, and you wanted her to come. Then tonight you were going to see Lisa.

Every one of the times that had gone before seemed to have been an enclosure for this one. It began on a lake with a poem and with the touch of a hand on your own hand holding the paddle. Then there was someone beside you, a person who knew so much more than you did that right off you were afraid. That night on the cliffside you were more afraid than you had ever been in your life because you knew that no matter how many times you warned yourself you could not turn away from the spaces before you. And now you were going to Lisa.

"I'm hungry," Ty said.

"Let's go to the kitchen and pick up some food before the counselors' meeting breaks up," Sara said. "Come with us, Abby."

"I'm too tired."

"But we'll be right back."

"You go ahead."

"What's wrong with you, anyway?"

"Nothing," Abby said. And as the others looked at her curiously, she went on, "I'm tired, that's all. The rest of you go along."

One after another the figures slipped from the cots and padded down the still path toward the dark hulk of Sky House. Abby lay very still. She had a sense of actually being tied to the cot but of being able to make the ropes go by wishing they would go. The night around her and the night inside of her got darker. This was like walking toward a place and hoping to find a light on the other side and knowing you would not find it. In a sudden, too-hasty movement she got up from the cot, pulling her dressing gown around her shoulders.

She went through the door and along the path where the pebbles no longer hurt her feet as they had when she first came here. Near the shore she paused, watching Mr. Mac on the dock swing the big lantern as he checked the canoes. And she shivered. This was like the cliff at White Water only she was looking up at the mountain instead of down into the valley. Only the lake, the mist, the moonlit sky. In her nostrils the smell of fresh water at night and of wet flowers. *I have a gift for you. I must see you alone.*

She turned, walking quietly under the black trees, coming like a ghost to Lisa's cabin, not calling, not whispering, walking more softly each moment, pausing at last near the door. In the moonlight the cots of the little girls who were asleep in the Dell stood like hospi-

tal beds. Lisa sat on the bed near the far ledge. Moonlight made the cabin almost as bright as if this were a
faint, early dawn.

"You're late," Lisa said.

"I couldn't come before."

"Why not?"

"I was afraid."

"Of what?"

"Of the others."

"You didn't tell them?"

"No—no."

Abby sat down on the bed as if she had been ordered
to sit there.

"I'm really afraid, Lisa."

"Silly child."

Beneath her Abby felt the sagging of a spring. She
sat for a long time watching the face in the moonlight,
then the instants began to close in on each other. All of
a sudden came a stupid desire to begin to talk about
those chimney sweepers, and wasn't it a bright angel
who had the key to the coffins? But she had not come
here for that. *I have a gift for you. I must see you alone.*

"I knew you were afraid," Lisa said.

"Nobody—" Abby spoke nervously—"nobody will find
us?"

"Not until the counselors' meeting is over."

"I'll be gone by then." And leaning closer, she asked,
"What do you want of me, Lisa?"

"Don't you know?"

On the cot Lisa sat straighter, her face bone-white in the moonlight. Watching, Abby wanted to become Lisa, and so desert herself. The need to shed her own self away was like a big wave pushing, always pushing. She herself was a sea, rolling and tossing in a tide of which she had no control. And suddenly she wanted to be away from these frightening waters.

"Maybe I'd better go now."

Lisa whispered lightly, "But I have something for you."

"Lisa . . ."

And the hand touching hers.

"The sapphire you've wanted."

Abby's mouth went dry.

"Your mother's——"

Lisa took the ring from her finger.

"I couldn't take it from you, Lisa."

"Why not?"

"A—a stone like that."

"The stone has nothing to do with it."

"I don't want it, Lisa."

"Are you sure?"

"I don't know."

The hand touched Abby's hand.

"You're cold."

"I'm all right."

But here in the cabin it did not matter whether she was all right or not. What mattered now, and all that mattered, was wanting suddenly to reach out and take the gift that lay ahead. This was a hard thing. This was like running to catch a present that was being thrown to you and not having any space to run. Even this cabin, open and bare as it was, seemed a close place.

"You've gone away," Lisa said.

"No—no."

"And you don't want the sapphire?"

"I—I——"

"You do want it then?"

"If—if you want me to have it."

She bent forward to watch this person who was so different from the one of daytime, so different from the one of any time. When Lisa slipped the ring on her finger she made no move. At a sudden noise like a scuffing both of them jumped up. Lisa moved quickly from across the room to the dresser by the door.

"What's that?"

"It's Mr. Mac on the dock."

"So it's only Mac." The words held relief.

Abby came to her.

"You really want me to have this?" Her whisper matched Lisa's of a little while before. "You're sure?"

"Of course." And the persistent whisper. "But you mustn't tell."

"Lisa, I don't——"

"Promise me."

The ring burned Abby's finger.

"I promise."

Lisa took her hand.

"Why, you're shivering. If you catch cold, you can't play your best in the basketball game tomorrow. And I want you to do well."

"I'll do well."

"Remember—don't wear your ring."

"Is it so important?" But Abby knew it was.

"You see, Gee Gee wouldn't like it."

Abby spoke in a high, faint voice.

"In the game, I'm going to make it up to Gee Gee for falling out on the trip to White Water."

"Make it up to Mother," Lisa said. "She still doesn't like the idea of your having gone on the trip when you were ill." And in that strange, soft voice: "Lead her along."

"I don't know how to do that."

"Let her see you again as you were that night in Cape Fear." She leaned closer. "I like to think of you as you were then."

"I'll play a terrific game," Abby said. "Lisa, I'll play for you."

Just at that moment the sounds came. Abby heard coming down the path the clip-clop, the terrifyingly familiar clip-clop, and it was as if God Himself were on the way. She forgot the ring, staring in terror hearing the clip-clop, the secret clip-clop, as if it were coming from far away, gaining with each moment. She looked out of the open front as if to hide in the clump of laurel at the side of the cabin, then stood stone still, caught in the glare of Gee Gee's searchlight.

"I've been looking for you," Gee Gee barked. "I wanted the big lantern but couldn't find it."

"Mac has it," Lisa said.

"Did you give it to him, Abby?" Gee Gee asked.

Abby did not reply. Gee Gee seemed really to see her for the first time.

"Why aren't you——" she asked. "Why aren't you in your cabin with the others where you should be?"

"She came down here to find out why Mac was on the dock," Lisa said.

"I think you're lying," Gee Gee said.

"Don't be ridiculous."

"Your mother won't think it's ridiculous!"

Lisa spoke too quickly.

"This doesn't concern Mother."

"You'd better tell me the truth." And to Abby, "What *are* you doing here?"

Lisa spoke again, her face in shadow.

"She just came down here to see me."

"But what for? What have you two been doing?"

"Abby just stopped by."

Gee Gee's words were like razor blades.

"You're lying, Lisa!"

"Why should I lie to you?"

"You have before."

"I don't know what you mean."

"Oh, yes, you do." She stepped closer. "And your mother will know, too."

Lisa's hand touched her throat.

"You wouldn't get her away from the meeting."

"Oh, yes, I would."

In the moonlight, Abby could see a vein swell in Lisa's throat.

"But all you could say is that Abby was out after taps."

Gee Gee quivered with anger and something more than anger as she swung toward Abby.

"Go back to your cabin. I want to talk to Lisa!"

Abby moved with uncertain steps toward the door.

"And Abby——"

"Yes."

As she swung around, the sapphire on her hand seemed to glow in the moonlight.

"I——" Seeing the ring, Gee Gee interrupted herself.

"Let me see your hand!"

Abby held out the hand as if putting it into the fire.

"Where did you get that ring?"

"That isn't your affair," Lisa said. The words were very faint.

"Your mother's ring!"

"You're going to tell her?"

"Of course I'm going to tell her."

As Gee Gee spoke, Lisa had begun to wear a look Abby

had never seen before. This was a frightened look, and
beyond it the look of a person deciding to do the best he
can for himself if it comes to that. This was a look that
gave a new dimension to Abby's distress. She kept glancing uneasily from Gee Gee to Lisa and back again. This
was a one-person look that made Abby sick at heart.

"I didn't ask Abby to come here," Lisa said suddenly.

"Why did she come?"

For a single moment Lisa became insolent.

"You're the one who seems to know. You're the one—
always." She swung around, giving Abby a secret be-
tween-us glance.

"Did Lisa give you that ring?" Gee Gee demanded
nothing less than the truth from Abby.

Stunned, Abby looked to Lisa for words.

Gee Gee's face was pale under the tan. "Did you give
her that ring, Lisa?"

Lisa did not reply.

"Did you?"

Lisa waited a long time before she spoke. And now
these were one-person words, not to change again.

"The ring was on the dresser," she said with a calm
that was like Deree's own. "If she picked it up, I didn't
see her."

Abby's heart began to bound like a rock rolling down-
hill. She did not understand this. She did not understand
any of it. The poem Lisa read to me, she thought, the way

she looked at me. And the gift. The sapphire on my finger. Now everything disappears, vanishes, goes in an instant. A lie, a lie, a lie of *memorable pomp*. The word "memorable" bounced crazily in her head. And now words were coming from Lisa's mouth.

"She's—been wanting the sapphire," Lisa said.

Gee Gee rose up taller.

"Did you take it from her, Abby?"

"I took it when she———"

"Abby!" Lisa's call was a warning.

"I came down here," Abby began, backing away, "because I wanted to see Lisa. I care for her and she cares for me. After we talked, she———"

Gee Gee threw the words like stone. "You're disgusting."

Disgusting, Abby thought. She blinked as if the moonlight hurt her eyes. "But I didn't steal." *Steal.* But you hid what you stole. You did not wear it openly. You did not leave it where anyone could see. And Lisa, now Lisa wore that look again.

"Did you steal it?"

The three of them stood there, caught in the silent space of the moment that comes before the one of rushing forward into ground you can never leave again. Gee Gee seemed to quiver all over like the arrow from one of her own bows. Abby was cold, cold. Then Lisa stepped forward from the shadow in which she had been standing.

"The ring was on the dresser," Lisa said again.

Abby wiped sweat from her forehead. In this strange conversation it seemed to her that somehow even more was at stake than whether the ring had been on the dresser or not. Or even whether she had taken it. She knew that Gee Gee had ideas beyond her own and that Lisa, too, had ideas she would never be able to follow. Could this meeting in the cabin have a terrifying, a permanent significance? *Promise me, promise me.* And Abby did not know.

"Did you take the ring?" Gee Gee asked.

When Abby did not reply Gee Gee took a long breath. "So it isn't a lie, after all."

Thief, Abby thought wildly, and the word was a bomb dropped before her. Now that it had gone off the whole sky must have blown to pieces . . . *thief* . . . *thief* . . . *promise me.* And there stood Lisa, calm in the moonlight, with a china look in her eyes. There stood Lisa looking as if no bomb had exploded at all. But Gee Gee, turning Abby's way, was shaken. Abby's face was drawn in the moonlight that slanted through the door.

"May I—may I go?"

"Shameless!"

"I'm full of shame for a lot of things I do." Abby was half choking. "Maybe more than I should feel."

"Are you bragging?"

"Let me—go."

"Unnatural!" Gee Gee said.

"Don't." Abby bent her head. "Don't."

"Don't." Lisa spoke as if coming from a long space away.

"Your mother will have to decide about this."

Suddenly Abby called out.

"You've backed me into a corner. Bullied me . . ."

And Gee Gee.

"Don't you dare talk to me that way!"

As Gee Gee's hand flicked out, whipping at the air, Abby felt that the hand had cut her face. Catching a glimpse of a Lisa who in the moonlight wore what might have been a smile, Abby had to catch herself against the door. This was like falling over a cliff with someone pushing you over and laughing about it. This was like being thrown into a black lake and knowing you were never going to see the surface again.

"Give me the ring you took from her," Gee Gee said.

Trying to pull it from her finger, Abby dropped the sapphire, then picked it up.

"Here," Gee Gee commanded.

"Before this is over," Abby began, in a faraway voice, "maybe you'll see——"

"It's over now," Gee Gee told her. "I'm going to Deree and report you for stealing." She looked into Abby's eyes. "And I can tell you this. You're going to get what you've been asking for."

"I've been asking for a lot of things," Abby said wildly. "And now I'll never get any of them."

She went out of the door, leaving Gee Gee and Lisa facing each other in the moonlight.

TWENTY-THREE

THE flags fluttered in the wind that came over the mountain on the afternoon that marked the start of Festival Week at Green Leaf. On the slope stood a set of flats being painted for the play in woodland colors. On the basketball court in front of Sky House, where the game would soon be played, were white chalk lines, newly placed boundaries for the players the visitors would be watching.

Near the court sat spectators who had already arrived. Some were parents, others golfers from the course at Linland, and others just people who happened to be vacationing near-by and had come to the camp to pass the time. The men in their caps and flannels, the women in their tweeds and Chanel, brought the world of a million miles away into the world of the camp.

In the dressing room at Sky House Abby stood up slowly, flexing her feet in the basketball shoes brought from Cape Fear. Knotting the sweater Jim had given her, and throwing it over her shoulders, she went out on the porch and stood looking at the court on which she would soon appear with the other players. Once she turned, sending a distressed glance toward Peg who was on the slope chatting with visitors from a newly arrived car.

"They're coming—they're on the way!"

Down the hill from Fir Lodge, where a rehearsal for the play had been in progress, came a group of troupers in dominoes wearing peaked hats on heads to which curls clung damply. As they went out on the basketball court and began their pre-game prancing, Peg left the slope and came to the porch. She stood by Abby a moment without speaking. Her voice when it came was strange.

"I must talk to you," she said.

Abby followed her into an inside reading room, waiting for the charge that was certain to come. Then, in watching Peg's face, she became aware of a despair behind the strangeness. For a long time the two of them stood there, each waiting for the other to say whatever must be said. Clenching her damp palms against each other, Abby forced herself to speak.

"Go on, Peg."

"I don't know what to say to you."

"Get it over."

Peg forced the words from her throat.

"About last night . . ."

Promise me, promise me . . . the words were in her like a black enchantment.

"So Gee Gee has told you."

"She told all of us." She stepped forward. "Did you tell Gee Gee you took that sapphire?"

"I didn't tell her anything."

Peg trembled.

"So Lisa told her that."

Abby did not speak.

"Did you—did you take it?"

Promise me, thief, promise me.

The counselor bent forward.

"This is important, Abby. Did Lisa give you the ring?"

"I can't tell you that."

"But you must."

"I can't."

"Tell me!"

"No—no!"

"Abby." The distress was everywhere. "You're ruining yourself. And not just for now. If you don't deny this, you'll take the disgrace away with you. You'll take it everywhere. If she gave you that ring, then you should know better than to keep quiet about it."

"I do know better."

"Then why——"

Abby wiped her face with her hand.

"Lisa asked me to come down there."

The counselor spread her hands helplessly.

"Why? Why?"

"I don't know why," Abby said. "Not yet, Peg. Really, I don't."

"I believe you. But if you won't defend yourself . . ."

"If I had stolen the ring," Abby said tensely, "I wouldn't have just worn it that way."

"Why didn't you say so?"

Promise me . . . promise me.

"I can't tell you, Peg."

"I tried to talk to the others about you last night," Peg said. "They didn't even hear me."

Abby faced up to her.

"Why did you call me in here?"

The counselor spoke it all in one sentence.

"Deree has changed the plans about the basketball game. You're not playing this afternoon."

"Not playing?"

"You can watch the game with me from the porch, if you like. Later, after supper is over, when she is free, Deree wants to talk to you at Tip Top Lodge."

"I'll—I'll go up there after supper."

"Abby," Peg said again, "why are you letting Lisa do this to you?"

"I've wanted something," Abby said dully. "Maybe I'd been trying to get it from Lisa. I don't know, Peg. It wasn't just the sapphire. I don't know. Honestly, I just don't know at all."

With the dark down over the camp, she started up the hill to Tip Top House. Touching the wool of her sweater, she began to think of Jim. He had been right. He had been right all along. And now he was as far away as that other basketball game in Cape Fear, and further back in time than any Cape Fear or any known place. If I had listened to him, she told herself, if I had believed him, maybe I would not have had to come to the place where I am.

The thought merged with the night noises of lake and hill as she neared Fir Lodge where the rehearsal for the play had begun again. At the porch she paused, an unwanted watcher before the window that opened on the players. Lisa in a diaphanous white dress was at center stage with the clown characters clustered around her. The speech came in liquid tones that seemed far divorced from the nighttime outside and from the harsh cry of a katydid.

> "Come, now a roundel and a fairy song;
>   Then, for the third part of a minute, hence,
>   Some to kill cankers in the musk-rose buds,
>   Some war with rere-mice for their leathern wings
>   To make my small elves coats, and some keep back
>   The clamorous owl that night hoots and wonders
>   At our quaint spirits. Sing me now asleep;
>   Then to your offices and let me rest."

Abby kept watching the scene as Lisa played it, the body graceful, the face white, imperious. She was so wonderful, it was hard to believe that she could be anything else. And maybe she wasn't. Maybe she had reasons of her own. . . . *promise me, promise me* . . . and would make them clear when the time came. But it was hard to understand. And it was hard to understand why she herself had accepted the charge without fighting it. *Thief . . . thief. . . .* the word sifted down through the leaves. It came to her in the night, and this time she could not shake free of it.

TWENTY-FOUR

THE room at Tip Top House was the same, and yet, since that first morning of coming here, a morning that might have been eons ago, everything had changed. Over there the shelf of books with the bright bindings at which she had sat and stared, waiting for Deree. Near the desk, Deree. Abby looked at her as if she were someone she had never seen before, or had seen but had not known. Not known at all.

"Last spring in Cape Fear," Deree said softly, "I was certain that at Green Leaf you could become the person I wanted you to be."

Abby looked away.

"I've earned my way with the lanterns," she said after a while.

Deree passed the words by as if they had not come.

"When camp began," Deree went on, "I was sure of you. But you have lost the path."

She went to the bookcase, and after a moment pulled a slim book from its place between two fat ones and replaced it with a volume that was more the same size. In the gesture it was as if she were rearranging and putting into their proper shelf thoughts that had been waiting all day for their true place in the pattern that had been forming behind her calm eyes. But in facing Abby again she seemed, to the watcher's surprise, to be not so much angry as dubious.

"Gee Gee tells me," she began, "that in Lisa's cabin last night you were bragging about what you had done."

"That's not true," Abby said.

Deree went from the bookcase to the desk, picking up the ring, staring at the mist-covered stone for a long time. Every move was deliberate, as if she were weighing far more than the object in her hand. Abby had the feeling that she herself was being balanced against the same forces that had begun moving last night in the moonlight of the cabin. And she also had a suspicion that no matter what she told Deree nothing about her own role would be changed now.

"Word of this has got round," Deree said.

I know, Abby thought. I know by the way they've been looking at me all day.

"The ring her father gave me." The light in Deree's eyes was light frost on glass.

Abby swallowed dryly. It came to her suddenly that this was more terrifically important to Deree than she had ever thought anything could be. Important to all of us, she thought.

"Did you—take it from her?"

Thief . . . thief. Abby looked from the fireplace to those waiting eyes.

"Did she give it to you?"

She could not reply.

"Answer me."

"I can't answer you."

Light flickered in the face.

"So she was telling me the truth," Deree said.

Mist and moon water, Abby thought suddenly. I'm more in mist than any of the others. Lost in mist near the edge of the water. Water good for getting drowned in, and yet somehow she had the feeling of having averted a drowning, if not for herself, for Lisa. If this were true perhaps even yet some time in the future she could find her way back to a safe place.

"You see, Abby"—Deree spoke softly—"as one grows older and the pattern repeats itself one has to know. With Lisa's father I had to face . . ." She was suddenly like a turtle crawling back into a hard shell. "One must know the truth."

"I—guess so." Abby was not following at all.

Deree, with a quick turn, said, "Did you brag about this to Gee Gee?"

"I'd never brag to a person like her." She felt the old hatred coming back. "She's the kind that just keeps hitting the dog till it falls down."

"She was frightened," Deree said. The words came slowly. "As I am."

What do they think *I* am, Abby wondered, starting suddenly to shiver. In that moment, if there had been any way at all to go back to last night in the cabin and start over again for herself, she would have gone. But it was too late. It was too late with Deree and always would be. To her surprise she heard herself making the attempt, with the words coming from far away.

"Why would I steal from Lisa?" she asked. "You see, I care for her."

"You . . ."

"I do care."

Deree was cold again.

"I don't understand you, Abby. I don't understand you at all."

Abby spoke out wildly.

"And I want a friend to care for me." She looked straight into Deree's glasslike eyes. "What's wrong with that? My mother used to tell me that love was all that mattered. I believed her. After she died, I kept holding on to that. It got me through the bad times. Now—now I don't even know whether she was right or not."

Deree looked at the sapphire lying on the table.

"You must start over again."

"Gee Gee cares for you," Abby was wilder than before. "I've seen her—I've watched her. You're the only person in the world she cares about at all."

"That's enough." Deree cracked the words.

From the desk she crossed the room to sit down in the big chair, the one with the pink cover that matched her cheeks. When she spoke again her voice was as cold as the wind on the mountain had been. And as Abby listened, her own face went as cold as if the wind had hit it. And all the time she simply did not believe the sentence Deree spoke.

"I think the only way is to send you home at once."

Abby's words were a whisper.

"What will you say to my father?"

"As little as I like it, the truth about you."

"I can't bear it."

"You should have thought of that."

"I love my father. I can't bear it."

"If you'd loved him, you would not have done this thing."

"Don't tell him, Deree."

"I'm afraid I must."

"But my scholarship to Steeple Hill. He's counting on

it." The future went slowly into a big black hole in front of her.

"You could have found everything," Deree said. "You could have found it here at Green Leaf."

Abby pushed dark hair away from her forehead.

"If I told you I did not take the ring from her," she began. "If I——"

"You've lied to me before. About Ida that night at Fir Lodge. I found that out."

So it *was* too late, even to take one step backward.

"Let me stay the week," Abby said, despising herself for begging. "Then people at home won't know. Then my father won't know. I'll have a chance . . ."

"Ida was ill," Deree went on. "And so are you, Abby. I simply cannot understand you." And with a quick breath, "You might have ruined my relationship with my daughter."

For a moment Deree sat without moving. Abby felt the cold more severe around her, but there was a difference. For suddenly, without any apparent reason, she knew that the wind had changed again, and that now it was hitting Deree, too. She sat quietly in her place by the wall until Deree began to speak in the tone she used when she held assembly in the Dell.

"For all that, it is my duty to help you."

Abby stood up.

"I hate you," she said. "You and your duty."

"Your self is what you hate."

"What do you really know about me?" Abby asked. "Standing up like God put you there. So sure of yourself. So sure of what I've done. I know what it is. At first I didn't know but now I do. You have to be the way you are—pretending all the time and not knowing it—or you couldn't get along at all."

"You are very ill," Deree said. "But perhaps if I keep you in my thoughts, if I do my duty and pray for you——"

"Let me out of here," Abby said suddenly. "I can't breathe in here. Tell my father. Tell anybody who wants to hear. But let me go home. Let me go!"

The other eyed her narrowly.

"I don't know about that, Abby. Not yet. In the end I'll do what I can for you. I'll think it over and do what's best." A look of being alone with some higher power came into her eyes. "I'll pray for you as if you were my own—as if you were Lisa."

She went into the bedroom. Abby turned, biting her lip to hold back the sobs that were filling her throat. *I'll pray for you as if you were Lisa.* She felt her way to the porch and picked up one of the lanterns lighted and left there by Mr. Mac. Her fingers like wire around the handle of the lantern, she moved down the path, pausing as the words of the Deree song drifted up from the cabins near the lake.

> "Oh, Deree Stephens,
> We hold high

Your pureness of heart.
We will hold it forever,
Though we depart.
Oh, Deree Stephens."

At the turn of the path near Fir Lodge, close to the spot where Ida had fallen in the fit on the ground, Abby paused and stood for a long time looking, as if some second self of her own might be lying there. To her left was a fir tree like a dark person. In front of it she stepped forward, smashing the lantern against the bark, and smashing it again and again, until the kerosene had sprayed everywhere over twisted wire. After a while she dropped the wrecked frame, brushed blood from a cut on her cheek, and then walked on down the hill.

TWENTY-FIVE

"Abby."

She turned to see Emmy beside her at the edge of the lake, with the trees everywhere like pushing shadows.

"What in the world are you doing down here by yourself?"

"I was listening to the frogs. You get so you know each one of them."

In a silence that was unusual for her Emmy sat down, staring into the blackness, shivering a little at the dolorous who-o-o of the owl that had joined the chorus of frogs and katydids. After a while the laughter from the girls lounging in their cabins during the free hour—it seemed to have begun a long time ago—became apparent. Emmy touched Abby's sleeve.

"You've been to see Deree, haven't you?"

"Yes."

"What did she say to you?"

"Nothing."

"A big nothing."

"She thinks I'm guilty."

"Why didn't you deny it?" Emmy wanted to know. "Why didn't you tell her the truth?"

Abby shook her head.

"Lisa gave you that ring, didn't she?"

"How did you know?" Abby asked dully.

"It had to be that way."

"Lisa asked me not to tell." Abby felt the ground with her finger. "I made her a promise."

"And so you lied for her."

The words came in a rush.

"When it was too late I wanted to take it back."

"It wouldn't have helped then," Emmy said.

"Deree may send me home before camp's over."

"Oh, Abby."

"She thinks I'm sick."

Emmy beat her hand with her fist.

"Lisa ought to be thrown off Stone Face."

"No," Abby said.

"Of course it's not the first time." Emmy looked at her sharply. "If that makes you feel any better."

"Nothing makes me feel any better," Abby said.

Emmy spoke softly.

"Larry knows her." And she added, "He's coming any day now."

"If Deree sends me away I won't be here when he comes."

Emmy sat for a long time looking at the dark.

"I don't think she'll send you, Abby."

"Why would she change?"

"Deree's a cold one. When she thinks it over she'll see how bad it would be for Green Leaf."

"That won't stop her."

"The thought of a scandal——"

"But there's one already."

"Not one for the outsiders." Emmy picked up a small stone, rubbing it between her palms. "And there's this to think about. Deree may still not quite believe you took her sapphire. Maybe she's pretending."

"She believes it."

"She has to keep face."

"The girls believe it," Abby said. "Ty, Sara, Bobby, Ellie—every single one of them. I can tell by the way they look at me."

"In a little while it won't matter to them at all," Emmy said gently.

"It will matter to me."

"At Steeple Hill this fall you'll forget."

"I'll never forget," Abby insisted.

"It will go with the summer. You'll be able to put it out of your mind—and put Green Leaf out, too."

"You're just saying that to try to make me feel better."

"No, really," Emmy said. And almost lightly, she added, "I wouldn't mind forgetting all about this place myself if it weren't for Larry."

"When did you say he's coming?"

"Any time now. And, Abby, if he stays at camp, I'll be tempted to stay with him."

"I knew you weren't coming home with me," Abby said. "I think I've known it all along."

Her voice trailed away as a burst of laughter from the cabin at the end of the line brought her smack back to the lake, making the thought of going home—with or without Emmy—seem preposterous. I have become two people, she thought. One of them is here and the other is off somewhere in the night trying to get home. In the darkness, with Emmy beside her, she hated herself for having been split apart this way. And there was no way of getting back together.

"I can't figure it out myself about Lisa," she said. "But it seemed to me—and still does—that both of us had to have the lie."

"Why do you think that?"

"I don't know." Abby rubbed her head again. "I had to do it and she had to let me."

"But why—why?"

"Maybe it had something to do with the way she feels about her father. He did give Deree the ring."

"Her father?" Emmy was suddenly sharp.

"I don't know. I don't know."

"Has Lisa talked a lot to you about her father?"

"She told me about him."

"Did she tell you he was better than anybody else?"

"Yes."

Emmy went hesitantly ahead. "Larry thinks Lisa has been badly hurt by her father's death."

"I know how that is. When my mother died——"

Emmy threw out the words.

"I'm trying to find out why this has happened. Maybe it is because Lisa cannot face the truth about her father, her feelings for her mother, or herself."

"But he was wonderful."

"For a time he seemed to be. But after Deree bought the camp and brought Gee Gee here—maybe even before that—something began to happen to him. They had to stand by and watch him break up and break up again."

"He—he lost his mind?"

"He made a great deal of trouble. Nobody could help him. When they decided to put him away, he killed himself."

"But Lisa thinks he was the most wonderful person in the world."

"He may have been that. But at the end it was very different. I think Lisa blames her mother for what happened to him. But she can't face it. She wants to hurt her mother. She doesn't even know how she feels. Some people are like that."

Abby sat very quiet. The lake was quiet, too, until a wind came off Stone Face to ruffle the water. So Lisa's father was not the man she thought he was at all. And neither was anybody else. Only you couldn't be sure even of that. Being sure had to be left for people like Deree. It belonged to them, and if you took it away—if you *could* take it away—nothing at all would be left for them. Abby sat unmoving, not excited, not angry, not uncertain, just cold—not anything at all.

"Do you feel any better?" Emmy asked.

Abby stood up.

"Everybody in the whole world is crazy," she said.

"That's nighttime thinking," Emmy replied.

The two of them walked down the path where the fir needles made a dark, soft rug for their feet. A stalk of goldenrod glowing in a shaft of light from a cabin showed buds that were further open than they had been the day Abby first noticed the flowers through the Infirmary window. The air, too, was different, with a bare hint of the frost that would come to these hills before the first cold touched the low country to which Abby soon might be returning.

"So you see," Emmy said again, "she won't send you home."

"It might be better if she did," Abby replied. "Then at least it would be in the open. Then I might find out the reason for it all."

TWENTY-SIX

THE August night outside of Sky House where the dance was drawing to a close held a damp thickness of late summer. The clouds of the afternoon had begun to move over the hills and into the hollows beyond the hills, dissipating themselves in the distance. But over the lake fog hung, bringing a chill to the air that was a hint of the autumn to come. In the big room where the girls were dancing, the windows were closed against the night and the fire in the great stone chimney blossomed everywhere, its flames dancing on the faces of the dancers.

"In less than a week it will all be over." Betsy Holt spoke to Emmy beside her. She spoke as if Abby, beside

Emmy, did not exist. "You'll be on your way home to Charleston."

Emmy spoke too calmly.

"I'll be on my way to Cape Fear with Abby."

Betsy shrugged.

"Well, I'd better get along and do a little work for the play." And slyly, "Everyone says Lisa is awfully good."

"So I hear," Emmy replied.

Betsy smiled at Abby.

"So you're staying with us, after all."

Not waiting for a reply, she turned to go, leaving Abby eying the girls who were still dancing, eying them and hating the curtain of shame that had begun to move over her face like water. She wanted to flee not only from Betsy—who had already gone—but from all the faces that seemed to her to be so curious and all to be staring in her direction. Peg came across the room through the crowd, gesturing an invitation to dance.

"No, Peg," Abby said.

"Come along."

"I can't."

Peg put an arm around her.

"Not much longer," she said as they moved out on the floor with the others. And then with warm laughter, "I've been dragging girls around this floor so long that I'll probably put a halter on Freddie and push him all over the floor at the fall cotillion."

Abby spoke halfheartedly.

"You'll fall right into his arms."

"Exactly." Peg giggled.

She moved out of the path of Ellie who was the unwilling partner of a junior camper who made Ellie into a giant. She went past the fireplace trying to get out of the sphere of Lisa who had come from play rehearsal to stand laughing with a group of counselors. The sound of Lisa's laughter scraped Abby like a knife. *I have a gift for you, promise me, promise me.* That sense of death was everywhere.

She managed to speak to Peg.

"My lanterns."

She broke away, and moved past the dancing girls to the back porch to begin the task of lighting the lanterns, holding the handles with fingers hard to control. After a moment she pushed up one of the shades, put a match to the wick, and watched the half circle of yellow light come alive from the kerosene. Inside the living room the girls had formed a big circle, their arms around one another as they sang.

> *"Deree Stephens*
> *We all love you,*
> *We revere you,*
> *Deree Stephens."*

The brightness of their faces reflected in the glow of the fire was part of a tableau from which now Abby knew herself to be forever removed.

At the edge of the porch, near the spot where the scraggly daisies had grown earlier in the season, Abby sat watching the hillside with the morning sunlight on it. Nearly the end now, with the play at last behind, and with only a few days until the honors, and the summer would be behind. She would go home—*thief, thief*—to her father and to a time when she would have to learn to live in a world that had got smashed into pieces.

Reaching over, she carefully picked up bits of glass from a lantern, broken like the one on the hillside, and thrown there after the night with Deree at Tip Top House. The glass fitted so neatly in her hand that it was almost as if by picking up the scattered bits she could form the pattern again, fitting it together and making it into what it had been before. One more fancy, she told herself, dropping the glass into the trash can. One more of too many fancies.

"Help me a little, Abby." She turned as Peg called from the storeroom where she was packing the costumes from the play that, like almost everything else here at Green Leaf, was at last behind.

In the room, with Abby beside her, Peg bent over an open trunk that was full of wigs, beards, and an old Gabriel's trumpet left over from the *Green Pastures* that had been the play of last year. It was as if the masquerade itself were here, but put away like one's dreams never to come back to life again.

"Let's jump up and down on this lid," Peg said.

"We'll break it."

"We'll break it or close it," Peg replied as the lid snapped shut under the pressure of their bodies.

Abby turned away to stand staring at the clothes hanging in the rack near the window where Peg had just finished arranging them in their places. These, drowned now deeper than the book of Prospero, hung wan in the light of the storage room—Snout, Starveling, Bottom—their costumes, like the midsummer-night's dream that was gone, tattered, worn, and, like the ass's head, poor reminders of another day. But the dress of Titania, cobwebby-white before her eyes, suddenly became as fresh as if it had never been touched or worn.

Peg lifted an eyebrow.

"First stop thinking about it," she said.

Abby evaded the counselor's stare.

"Will you stay here to help Deree close up camp?" she wanted to know.

"If I stayed one extra day I think I'd die," Peg replied.

She tossed her head in sudden laughter. "I'm sick of smelly flannels and woolly gabardine, of fog and crafts and exercises on a damp hill. I want a dance floor with dim lights and music. I want a red strapless dress and Freddie's arms around me."

Again she looked at Abby.

"You'll be dancing," she said softly, "in Steeple Hill. I went up there once for the fall germans with a friend of mine from the law school. What a time! What a place! Good-looking boys everywhere. With convertibles. And ready to snap the top down over the head of a pretty girl like you."

"It's no good," Abby said.

Peg touched her hand.

"Your Jim."

"He hasn't written me," Abby replied.

She walked away to the steps, staring out over the lake with its black waters. Like the world of last spring, Jim had never even existed at all.

From the path Lisa came up the steps to stand staring at Abby with expressionless eyes. At the door Peg locked the storeroom, tossed the key lightly in her hand as if to say, *that's that,* and went along down the steps to the path. Maybe Peg's right, Abby told herself, if I could only make myself believe her. This lake, these hills, these people, all can become last year's dream. Then Lisa stepped closer.

"You've been hiding from me." The voice was worn and sharp.

"I don't want to talk to you," Abby said.

The other spoke with a new brusqueness.

"I'm sorry it had to go the way it did."

"Please, Lisa."

"You didn't tell Mother."

"There's nothing to say."

"What did you tell her?"

"Let's leave it the way it is."

"You lied for me," Lisa said softly.

"I suppose you could call it that."

"For me."

Abby spoke savagely.

"Whatever I did was for myself."

In Lisa's cheeks the color was higher than before, a vivid, painted pink.

"She very nearly sent you home."

"But she didn't."

"The girls despise you."

Abby swallowed hard.

"Emmy doesn't."

"But she's not going to Cape Fear."

"She may."

"Her aunt doesn't think she should. Mother phoned her, you know."

So Miss Matthis would know. *Thief, thief.* And her father—her father?

"Of course you won't get honors on Fire Night," Lisa went on.

"I hadn't ever expected them." But it was a lie.

Lisa bent closer.

"Mother and Gee Gee are still angry."

"Let them be," Abby said.

Without taking a step, Lisa began a subtle process of backing away.

"Let them be," Abby said again.

Lisa's cheeks had white in them.

"Don't be vicious."

"I've got to find out something." Abby might have been talking to herself. "I've got to find out who I really am. I'm trying to find out if I am——"

"Whatever you are, don't blame it on my mother."

"If I'm wicked, I want to know it."

But Lisa was not hearing.

"Mother's a fine woman. She's making her whole life out of the ideal of helping other people."

"Did she help your father?"

Lisa caught her breath.

"You got that from Larry!"

"It doesn't matter where I got it. But that day on the lake, and all the other days, you made me believe your father climbed a ladder that went right up to the sky. And your mother. You never told me how afraid of her you are. You must hate her."

"Damn you!" Lisa said.

"All right." Abby spoke wearily. "Let's leave it there." And then with a dying gust of anger, she said, "You never told me he killed himself."

"It's a lie."

"All right," Abby said. "It's a lie."

She began to watch Lisa as if from a great new distance. It was all gone. The Lisa of that first day, smiling on the dock: dusk on the lake with the leaves like a wood to lie down in along the shore where the light was fading. It had died that night in the cabin, and perhaps before then. The closeness the summer had brought was something she could never believe in again.

"You bored me from the first moment I met you," Lisa said suddenly. "A girl like you."

Abby turned, taking a lantern shade from the shelf where the extra materials were kept, and trying to rub it clean against her sleeve. So it had been nothing from the beginning. And her belief in Lisa was nothing. Everything had to go. You knew that the first time you saw a leaf or a person die. But what stabbed at her heart was having the time at the camp, so radiant in prospect, turn ugly and black like the smudge on her fingers from the shade held in her hand.

"Would you really like to know what's the matter with you?" Lisa asked.

Abby bent her head.

"You care too much. You want too much from people and are too open about wanting it. You don't have any defenses. You betray yourself and make it easy for other people to betray you."

Abby spoke in chipped accents.

"You're right."

"I had to do what I did to protect myself. But you didn't have to let me do it."

"I'm learning." Abby stood straighter. "But it won't be easy."

"What won't be easy?"

"Turning myself into a liar like you!"

The slap came hard, quick, leaving a great red patch on Abby's face. It was just a slap, nothing more, but this was the mark of one moment on all of the moments of the summer. And it hurt. As Lisa turned away, walking with fast steps up the path toward Tip Top House, Abby sat down near the lanterns and touched her cheek. Funny, but it seemed now to be the other way around, as if she had been hitting Lisa.

TWENTY-SEVEN

LARRY came back to the camp, came over the mountains early in the morning of the day that would bring the Fire Night Ceremony. He came with the sun on him, driving a borrowed convertible in fast time from his friend Jake Dean's summer place at Cray Lake across the hills. From the Craft Shop, to which she had come before starting the schedule for this last day, Abby got a brief glimpse of him as Larry parked the car near the cabin on the slope, his cabin. With the unfinished rug

she was taking home held in her taut hands, she watched
the arrival. He came into the camp wearing sunburn. He
came into the camp laughing.

Putting down the rug, she stood at the window watching the car after its occupant had disappeared up the hill.
No meeting of Larry at Flat Rock this time, with too
much talk on the ride back over the hills from the Ridge
Shop. No errands left to do, no lanterns left to buy.
There was no assembly in the Dell and the mornings of
memorable pomp were just mornings you did not want
to remember. As he came into camp that day, Abby
thought of him as a person from a better world.

He came for a picnic in the Dell, for the Fire Night
Ceremony lying ahead, and after it the departure. Tomorrow the girls would be leaving the camp to go home
by air, by train, by car. The canoes would be racked on
the dock, the windows of Sky House would be shuttered
against the cold, the horses would have gone from the
stables to Flat Rock for their winter quarters, and the
camp itself would have become a shell. But this morning
the camp was still itself, a heightened self with the Fire
Night Ceremony lying ahead.

Not ahead for Abby but for her, as for the others, the
end of the summer was really here, with the time gone
by, past and done. The picnic lunch, one more swim in
the lake, and then, with dusk, the procession of girls
marching toward the appointed place would begin. Sud-

denly aware of the rug she had been holding in her hands, Abby placed it in a box and walked out of the Craft Shop along the path to her cabin.

"What you got there, Abby?"

It was Mr. Mac, climbing down from the truck in which he had brought the ice cream for the lunch from Flat Rock.

"A rug I was making for my aunt. Only I didn't ever finish it."

"Anyway, you're taking a little bit of the mountains home with you."

"A little bit."

"Big day today," he said.

She turned to go.

"Everybody's having visitors," he kept on.

"So I hear."

"You, too, Abby."

She stared at him dully.

"You're going to have a visitor from home."

My father, she thought. He'll know.

"Well, ain't you interested?"

"Is—it——"

"A fellow named Brandon. I run across him in Flat Rock at the Ridge Store. He's on his way to Furlong. Hitchhiking. Got a ride from the coast."

She did not speak.

"He's coming over this afternoon."

Holding the box hard, she walked away. And around the cardboard her hands were trembling.

She sat with Larry on the float but she watched the shape of Fir Lodge on the hill where the visitors would come. In a little while now it would be time. What did you say? How did you greet a person who came into a world that was dead? What did you say of yourself? What could you say?

Beside her, Larry glanced her way. Then pulling his long legs up under him, he stared again at the Cove where the bonfire was being laid for tonight's ceremony. In the circle the great pile of logs, and above it the space into which the doe—so far away—had disappeared. When Larry spoke, it was in what seemed to her to be a deliberately unconcerned voice.

"I see Mac's getting the logs ready."

She followed his glance.

"A lot of logs."

"Oh, Mother makes quite a thing of the Fire Ceremony." He laughed easily. "I've always thought of it as a kind of Green Leaf *Götterdämmerung*."

"Sounds big," Abby said.

"Well, whatever you call it, she'll have a good night for her blaze. Cold."

Beside him Abby shivered.

"I'd better go."

He spoke soberly.

"You're having a visitor?"

"Yes."

"It's not quite time yet."

"You knew about Jim," she said. "How did you know?"

"Mac told me." He looked away from her toward the shore. "Emmy tells me you've been having a very bad time."

"Your mother doesn't think so."

"Mother's not too happy about it."

Abby looked at the stretch of water that lay between her and the mountain, watching the reflection of Old Stone Face. It was like a green path leading down from heights you could never reach again. If Deree was not happy, she thought, she would never show it, even by a twitch in that calm lake of a face. But maybe nobody was happy, after all. Maybe that was the thing you had to learn before you could learn anything else. And then you could put the summer behind you.

For it was dead. And the people of the camp were dead. As dead as the way people looked when you put them into the last little box, as dead as her mother had looked that last day in the coffin. Lisa was the deadest of all, and yet that face kept looking up at her from the water lilies. A ghost face, and had been that from the beginning. So it had not died with the others, it had only seemed to die. Again the cold came, boring into Abby.

"That's going to be some fire," Larry said again. "But I don't think I'll be here for the show."

"Why not?"

"I'm going back over to Cray to see Jake."

"I'm attending the ceremony," she said. "But I'll not be here, really."

Saying it made her feel better. It made her feel safe, as if in a way she had managed to crawl part of the way back toward the real world. To speak out loud was to try to shake free. It was a way of moving back into the past at least far enough to achieve a faint resemblance to the Abby Gregory of last spring. As Abby glanced up, Larry put the question.

"Will you tell this Jim what happened to you here?"

"I don't know."

Larry pretended to watch a swimming camper who circled a red buoy near a lily patch and afterward headed back for the dock, splashing lustily. Pretending with him, Abby tried to put away her shame, at least for a little while. She tried to begin making herself into the person Jim would be coming to the camp to see. And now Larry was looking at that person.

"This camp was never the place for you," he said.

"Last spring"—she spoke hesitantly—"I was certain it was the only place in the world for me."

"That was asking too much."

"I've asked too much, and cared too much," she told him, putting her hand to her forehead. "What kind of man was your father, Larry?"

"He was a person like the rest of us," Larry said. "Trying in the best way he knew to get through the process of living—and in the end of dying."

"Did his death change Lisa?"

"I think it did."

"I just wanted to know."

She pushed back a lock of hair as if to push away a disenchantment that would never lend itself to the spoken word. Suppose she said, "Lisa made me into a liar but I was one already." But you did not say that kind of thing. And Deree, his mother? What of her? Suppose Deree did want to keep her own little paradise intact. Suppose she did stamp on other people so that they could never ruin it for her. *Thief . . . thief. . . .* Was it Deree's right? She couldn't ask Larry. Or wouldn't.

"You'd better stop it, Abby," he said.

"Stop what?"

"Being so interested in the girl you love."

She looked at him with the eyes of a person who has been caught in the act of stealing.

"She's you," he said.

He slipped from the float and swam toward the shore with a long stroke. Looking up, she suddenly saw her own image everywhere. In the sky, in the Dell where the fire was being made ready. She saw it everywhere. It seemed to be in her and at the same time outside of her, filling up the world and leaving no room for anything else. She suddenly felt a thrust of anger at the whole world, at the God who might have made it and thrown her into its spaces.

"Abby," Emmy called from the shore, where Larry had joined her, and beckoned toward Fir Lodge where the visitors had begun to arrive.

"Come along, Abby, it's almost time!"

TWENTY-EIGHT

AT THE Lodge she looked toward the slope where Ida had sprawled that night. In her once again was that terrible sense of unreality. It was as if the speckled sunlight of the afternoon, the circle of the hills, and the very world itself had become nothing. This nothing stretched out past the tumbling hillocks, over lake and pasture, embracing the plains, and merging at last into the beaches Jim had left behind him to visit her here. She turned suddenly, wondering if he was coming at all.

It was past the hour now, with the visitors scattered over the camp, some of them talking with Deree and others gone down the hill to the court where they mingled with campers and counselors. Here in the Lodge it was silent and so lonely that it made her afraid. She turned and went across to the porch looking down toward the gate. As she watched he came through the gate, moving with quick steps, walking like a person late for an appointment.

"Well, I found you."

When he held out his hand the nothing around her began to dissolve. He was real, he had arrived. And now he was here on the porch, tossing his coat into that chair. Abby kept looking at him. His hair was shorter, his shoulders were heavier, but he was a known person. He had always brought that feeling of being known with him, and now he brought it again.

"I was late with my ride," he said.

They sat down on a bench, two stiff figures.

"The—the visiting time isn't a very long one," she said. "I hoped you'd get here sooner."

"My ride was late," he said again.

"How long can you stay?"

"I'll have to start out again tonight."

"It's a long trip for such a little time."

He spoke roughly.

"Football practice starts tomorrow. I have to be at Furlong by noon."

She did not look at him.

"So this is your camp, Abby."

"This is Green Leaf."

"Quite a layout."

Abby looked at the lake. She put her hand to her head as if to brush away a persisting image.

"Pretty," she said.

His eyes were on her body.

"Very pretty."

Aware of his stare, and too aware of him beside her, she was more afraid than in the aloneness of a little while ago. In a moment—she knew, she could tell—he was going to touch her. As his hand moved she was frightened by his insistence, shocking and powerful. Here was the sense of being caught in a new trap, one of the strongest steel. She wanted to be caught, wanted it desperately, even while the fear was on her.

"Abby," he said, "what's wrong?"

"Nothing."

"Didn't you want me to come see you?"

"Of course I did."

"You haven't written very much."

She looked at the lake and at the cliff striking into the sky beyond it.

"I've been in trouble, Jim."

He sat very still.

"Trouble?" he asked.

"With the camp."

"I thought you were their best girl."

"Bad trouble."

"What is it?"

"They think I—I took something."

"Took something?"

"From a girl," she said. "A sapphire ring."

"Oh, for God's sake."

For a moment it was as if he would throw back his head and send laughter out to strike the trees, the cabins, and the faces of the people on the slope below. Then, aware of the pallor in Abby's face, he sat straighter on the bench than before. After a while he put his hand over hers.

"Do you want to talk about it?"

She opened her lips but could not speak to him any more than she had been able to speak to Larry on the float a little while ago, for none of this was as simple as it seemed to be. There beside Jim, with his hand over hers, she suddenly had a sensation of having reached out to take something far more important than any ring. And it was wrong. The wrong stretched far back, past the remembered face of her mother, deep into time, deep into desires that loomed fearfully.

She spoke too calmly.

"I haven't done anything wrong."

His eyes were puzzled.

"Why would anybody think you did?"

"Somebody accused me."

"And you denied it."

"No." She bent her head. "I did not deny it."

He swallowed dryly.

"Why, in God's name, didn't you?"

"I'm not sure." *Promise me, promise me.* "I've still got to find out why."

Jim shook his head as if to shake an ache away.

"Who—who accused you?"

"Mrs. Stephens' daughter," she said. "I—I——" She could not go on.

He stared soberly at Abby.

"They believed her because of who she is?"

Abby spoke reluctantly.

"It's not that simple, Jim."

He took her by the shoulders, forcing her to look at him.

"Did you take the ring?"

"She gave it to me."

"Then it *is* simple," he said. "A liar like that ought to be——"

"But, Jim, I have to tell you. I——"

He looked at her anxiously.

"Abby, must we settle this ring affair now?"

She did not reply.

"Is there anything I can do? Anything now?"

"Nothing."

"Then let's put it behind us until later," he said. His eyes were more anxious than before. "I came a long way, Abby. I don't have much time."

She looked at the sun that was lower now in the sky.

"It *is* late."

"We'll still have a few hours together."

"No, Jim," she said. "You'll have to go when they tell you to go. When the gong rings."

"Oh, no, I won't."

"You'll make trouble."

"There's no law against my being here," he told her angrily. "What kind of a joint is this, anyway?"

"It's the big night," she said nervously. "They're getting ready for the Fire Ceremony. Everybody has to leave except the campers."

The laughter came in his eyes.

"Fire Ceremony. Are you the chief?"

"I'm nothing."

"What time is this ceremony?"

"Just after dark."

"And you have to go?"

"Everybody has to go."

He had her hand again.

"You say you have nothing to do with it?"

"Nothing at all."

"I'll stick around. I'll go on out to the road when the visitors leave. Then later I'll meet you."

"Jim, you can't."

"Where will you be?"

"I don't know."

"Let's see." He looked toward the chair where his coat lay. "I'll forget my coat and have to come back for it. Then, if they find me . . ."

"You can't."

He had her in his arms.

"This is our only chance. Where will you be?"

"I'll be—" her breath came faster— "I'll be up on the slope with the others."

"I'll get lost looking for my coat, and wander down toward the fire." He planned it as he spoke. "You leave the others and come to meet me."

"But I——"

He was close again.

"Where shall we meet?"

Her breath came fast.

"By the big fir tree over there. The one with the white scar on the trunk."

While he looked at the tree, fixing its position in his mind, the gong sounded the end of the visiting hour. Up the hills came the parents and friends, past Tip Top House toward the parking lot where the cars waited. Jim stood for a moment still watching the big fir, then went on down the path to the lake road. Watching those long, certain steps, Abby almost became a person for whom the world was real again.

TWENTY-NINE

THE honor girls in the Fire Night procession walked past the cabins and along the shores of the lake under dark trees. In the moments before the final ceremony began a quietude had come from the hills, a quietude that seemed to be here from eternity and for eternity. From her place not far from the fir tree with the white scar, Abby sat staring at the campers who were carrying their candles, shielding their lights carefully until they reached the open space in which Deree would make the awards.

> *"Follow, follow, follow the gleam,*
> *Banners unfurled*
> *O'er all the world.*
> *Follow, follow, follow the gleam*
> *Of the light that shall bring the dawn."*

Many little lights flickered in the clearing, a few fireflies and others from the flashlights of the girls who would be spectators of the Ceremony. Now they were settling themselves in groups a little lower down on the slope. They sat on ponchos or blankets in dark little clumps that hardly looked like people. All the campers watched those with the candles who were now almost at their designated spot near the fire.

> *"Follow, follow, follow the gleam,*
> *Standard of worth over the earth,*
> *Banners unfurled o'er all the world."*

They wore the camp uniform with a band on each arm to show each figure as separate and marked apart. But for that all were alike. All quiet. No banners to-night. No flags, no cheers to mar the tone of the ritual. The chosen girls, ending the procession, sat down near the fire from which the flames began to leap as if they would never stop until they had burned out the sky.

"Abby," Peg called from the darkness, "I'm over here. I've saved a place for you."

Abby went by Peg, touching the counselor's sleeve. She kept going, up the slope to the chosen tree, away from the others, shielded from them by the shadow of a cabin. She was out of the flicker of the flames now, a person apart from the circle and the girls who sat near it. After a moment she turned, seeing a dark form, and then realizing that it was Jim beside her.

"I've got to get my coat, Abby," he said. "Wait for me."

"Jim, do you think——"

He might not have heard her at all.

"I'll be back."

When he had gone she sat watching the fire below.

Along this part of the hill the fir trees lay like a fence, head high between this spot and the crowd of campers on the slope. Beyond the tops of the trees the firelighter, whose job was now done, went to the edge of the circle. The blaze that was so much a part of this ceremony leaped even higher than before. Abby waited, thinking of words Deree had spoken in the Dell one day a long age ago. *I made no vows but vows were then made for me* . . . and the dedication had changed with everything else.

"We are here for our night of consecration," Deree was beginning. The words came up the hill faintly.

"Together we give reverence to this fire which represents the spirit of God."

The fire keeper tossed a handful of pine-scented baubles into the flame. With added color the fire leaped green, pink, red, spurting upward, placing into spotlight the faces of the honor campers and of the counselors who were a part of the ceremony. Abby thought suddenly of Ida, gone without leaving a vacant place. For a moment the memory of that face pushed away the thought of Jim.

> *"Fire, fire, pure and bright,*
> *Lead us upward to the light,*
> *Leaping mystery of fire,*
> *Cleanse our hearts of dark desire.*
> *Fire flaming upward strong,*
> *Purge our hearts of secret wrong."*

Abby bent forward, almost drawn into the circle. *Make free our hearts from secret wrong.* What was this thing she dreaded, intangible but no less real because no eye could behold it? What was this thing that separated her—for she was separate again now—from the others, from Ellie with her baby-doll smile, from Bobby whose cheeks never carried a stain, from Ty with her easy sanctity—and from all the rest? Thief, thief, and more than thief. Staring at the fire, she had the eyes of an alien, a stranger.

"Fire, fire, swift and bright . . .
Bring us strength to do the right."

She looked up at the sky where for a moment a moon came through a sheaf of clouds to hang there like a great ball toward which you could leap, leaving everything that was here, and being caught up into heaven itself. As suddenly as it had come the ball of a moon disappeared. You never get free, she thought. If you go after the moon, you fall down against a stone. If you try to dream, you smash the dream to pieces the way you smash a lantern shade.

"All of you, my girls." Deree's words were fainter than before.

Lisa came from behind a shelter of boughs and stood near her mother holding the badges for the honor girls in her hand. In the setting of this ceremony, Lisa wasn't a person at all. She stood by the fire as a figure that went with her mother, that belonged with her mother. She was apart from everything, from the girls who sat on the slope and from Abby on the slope above them.

"The bonds we have together will always tie us," Deree said. "And now the names of the honor girls."

All her girls, Abby thought bitterly. They knew right from wrong, up from down, black from white. They knew the answers to the questions that she herself did not even know how to ask. As Deree began to read the names Abby walked farther up the hill, blocking herself completely away from the figures on the slope and those in the circle. Where is he, she wondered in panic. Has he left me? And will he never come?

"I almost didn't find you," Jim said. "It's so damned dark."

He held her arm.

"This is the way."

They retreated from the firelight along a track that led to a sheltered place blocked away from the ritual below. They sat close to each other, seeing the fire only above the trees in the distance. On the lake a bullfrog made a sound that was like a satiric belch. Once a shower of sparks fell like stars. From the campfire the singing died and rose and died away again. From a long way off came the sound of a whippoorwill. In the darkness Jim spoke quietly.

"Abby," he said, "what you were trying to tell me this afternoon is important, isn't it?"

"Yes." *Thief, thief. More than thief.*

"Tell me now."

"I can't, Jim. Not now."

His voice came out deep, like her father's. "We'll try to work it out together."

She did not reply.

"What is it? What's wrong?"

Watching the flames leaping to the sky, she shivered. In the flames the faces of the girls mocked her. And Lisa—Lisa was laughing.

"Forget those people down there," he said suddenly. "You've got to forget them."

"But, Jim——"

"It's you and me, Abby."

They sat close beside each other on the slope. Far below them the red flames seemed to die in the dark. His arms were around her, blocking away all that had been. For the first time she began to be free of the swift fire, the singing girls, the lake beyond the girls, with the mist and water lilies drowned in the night. Now Jim's hand was on her breast and she did not push it away. She turned to him as if for shelter.

"It's you and me," he said again.

"Jim——"

"We're in our own country. Under the pines."

"Jim, darling."

"I've been waiting so long."

"Please——"

If he heard her he gave no sign. Instead, he pulled her to him in a dark embrace, and in her body a movement of happiness began. Maybe this was what she had been waiting for all along. Maybe all the rest was going to move away. The accusing faces, the cold cliffside, the mists of the camp were going now. The moon itself was dying on the wet pillow of the earth. In the protecting dark, with his hand on her bare breast, she whispered entreaty.

"Be good to me, Jim."

What she would not do for him last spring was done now in the dark in these woods that were like a little house. Here were the old fears and the stronger desire. Beneath her the slope and above her his body. He's an animal, she thought, a nice animal, and I am here on the wet earth beneath him. This was the time from which there had been no escaping, the wild blood in the body, the deep dark of the embrace. It was all here, all now.

In the dark he was close, close, his breathing muffled, broken, and hers a cry.

THIRTY

ON THE hills above the station at Flat Rock from which the girls were departing the leaves were not green any more. Or at least not the tender green they had been in June when Abby arrived in this same place on her way to the camp. Now the leaves on the trees near the track were a dusty, dull, end-of-the-summer color, with some red showing on the sumac and the dogwood. But Abby did not see the leaves, for her mind was too filled with images.

She saw Deree Stephens' face as it had been that first day, and saw it again as it had been this morning in the moment of farewell. Deree had been as polite in the moment of parting as in the moment of meeting last spring. Abby saw the face, the cheeks as pink as the tea roses sometimes brought from Mr. Mac's garden to grace the space on the mantel of Tip Top House.

"Good-by, Abby," Deree had said. And stiffly, "Have a good journey home."

There in the station, alone in the middle of the push-

ing crowd of girls, Abby put a fist to her eye. She saw
Lisa, and heard Lisa's aloof words that had been an echo
of Deree's. *Pleasant journey.* In that last moment she
had again recognized the Lisa of other times as a dream
image, but one in which the real world had been dissolved. The dream image had been most alive that day
on the lake, and then vivid again in the cabin before
Gee Gee's visit and the fright it brought. The image
had come back to life again—even though by then it had
changed its face—on that day of the hard slap. As Abby's
clenched fingers opened to touch her cheek where the
mark still lay, a trainman called out to Mr. Mac.

"That your last batch of campers, Mac?"

"Yep. All here."

"Ten minutes and we'll get under way."

In the rough tones Abby heard an echo of Jim's words
of last night—*Good-by, Abby, I'll see you in Steeple
Hill*—and saw his face in the darkness on the hillside.
She touched her dress to be certain that the collar hid
her kiss-bitten neck. *Good-by, good-by—I'll see you in
Steeple Hill. I'll see you in the fall.* One more kiss with
his mouth hard on hers, and he had gone.

See you in the fall. In the fall the trees at the camp
would be spangled with scarlet and lacquered with gold.
The cove where she had seen the doe that first morning
would lie silent. Nothing was ever going to be what it
had been, and it was right now that it should not be.
But it was hard to think of the falling leaves and of a

doe that would never swim the lake again or climb safely into the green haven of the forest.

"Well, Abby."

"Hello, Mr. Mac."

She came back to the station to see the CHEW RITE TOBACCO sign turn into a bright red frame for Mr. Mac's face.

"You're on your way," he said. "When you get to Cape Fear give your father my best. And be sure to send me those sea oats."

"I will."

"Going to miss you."

"You'll have Emmy and Larry for a while," she said.

"You mean they'll have each other."

Abby bent her head.

"I missed Larry in the rush this morning before we left," she said. "I wanted to see him." But she really had not wanted to see him.

As Mr. Mac walked away with long crane strides the conductor called out for the girls to begin to take their places on the train. On the tracks the special cars looked shiny and impressive in contrast to the mountain-dusty engine. Abby moved up the steps of the north-bound car that would be connected with the express an hour away at the Junction.

> *"Oh, Green Leaf*
> *We are bound to you. . . ."*

On the steps of the car she looked at the faces of the singers like a person hearing words in an unknown language. Around her were girls, some gay with laughter, some sober-eyed, some already as expectant for home as if camp had never existed for them. Ty, Sara, Ellie, —looking at each other and looking away. Abby did not sing with the rest.

> *"Going back,*
> *Going back,*
> *Going back to town and fall.*
> *Going back,*
> *Going back,*
> *We'll still hear Green Leaf's call."*

Looking at the girls again, she thought that this was part of a funny time, this mountain station with the lazy watchers, these campers in their town dresses instead of shorts. There they were with their arms around one another, their faces like those of calves bleating at the moon. Maybe all time was a funny time. Maybe all faces of friends became strangers. Maybe every hour would be harder to understand than the hour that had gone before.

"All right, girls. Get aboard."

The trainman moved his arms stiffly. The train snorted then as if not wanting to obey his command but being forced to start down the mountain. In this moment Abby turned for a last look at the hills above Flat Rock. In the instant of watching a shadow on those hills she felt the black shadow in herself, but a streak of sunlight thrust its way just then over the mountains like a sword cutting away at the dark. As she started up the steps, someone called out to her.

"Abby!"

She turned to see Larry coming toward her, pushing his way through the crowd, looking taller than he was. She wanted suddenly to run away from Larry as from all the others, going faster than any train could go, right straight across that mountain, leaping like the doe over the ridge into gentler country, never pausing until she came to Cape Fear. Home is the place where sometimes you have to hide.

"I wanted to say good-by," he said, and put his arm on hers. "Take it easy."

He turned away as the last order for boarding the waiting train was shouted by the conductor. Like a sleepwalker Abby sat down in the coach where the girls were waving final farewells to a mountaineer who stood under a shed near the Ridge Shop not caring whether anybody left or stayed. The last Abby saw of Larry was that long frame disappearing into the small depths of a truck.

"So it's over."

She turned to see Peg, red hair hidden under a little knitted cap. The counselor patted the seat beside her.

"I'd better go up to the other car, Peg. For Cape Fear. It isn't very long to the Junction."

The counselor leaned forward.

"The best of luck, Abby. Try to forget what happened

at the camp. Start from here. Believe me the days at Green Leaf are already just a little scrap of paper in time."

Abby moved down the aisle toward the Cape Fear car. A little scrap of paper in time—with a great big word on it. She passed one camper then another, dark heads, red heads, strangers in city clothes that had been taken from camp closets and still smelled of cleaning fluid. She thought of her lanterns, and wanted them again. Of all the camp, the lights on the back porch were the only things she wanted to take home with her. But you could not choose what you would take.

"Call me, Abby"—Ty was patronizing—"if you ever come to the city."

The city, the city. Perhaps there will still be some place she could escape what had happened, lose the stamp of it and never be hurt again. A city where she could become the self she wanted to be, moving among the piercing towers and glittering stones that had seemed so near in the spring. That day on the lake when Lisa had spoken of the city came back to her. Somehow Lisa had managed to make the city become an avenue alive with lights. Were its bright jangles dulled forever?

"Good-by, Ty," she said, and walked away.

In the Cape Fear car she sat down and folded her hands. As she looked through the window the sense of loss was apparent in her face and in those brown eyes that kept looking, looking, still hoping to find what no longer existed. The loss was apparent in the way in which she held her body against the seat, casual, but casual by an effort, as if even after last night she could not be herself and yet could not yet become someone else.

Good-by, Abby, I'll be seeing you in the fall. The time on the hillside pushed its way into the train. He's an animal, she thought again, a nice animal. And the odor of his body merged into the smell of wet earth. *We're at home under the pines. Be good to me, Jim, be good to me.* As she stared at the green black of the floor of the car it became the earth of the hillside. And here was his face again, not to be pushed away.

After a little while she looked up to see girls' faces framed in the window of the car on the next track. They were still strangers. Gone away as the moments on the lake and on the hillside were gone. All gone, all dream-dressed. The girls would always be alien. These people whose hands she had touched, whose songs she had sung, whose lanterns she had kept burning during the night. Here they were, faces patterned behind smudged panes, mouths open in silly array like sheep.

> *The last doe ran across the brook,*
> *The keeper fetched her back with his hook,*
> *Where she is you may go and look,*
> *Among the leaves . . .*

Among the leaves, Abby thought, and Jim's face loomed among the faces of the girls. From the other cars they were screaming good-bys to one another now, cry-ing out in voices that were as meaningless as the chirp-ing of birds heard in early morning when one is only half awake. It seemed to her, suddenly, that the girls were birds, flown out from their grove of leaves, growing smaller in passage, screaming and crying as they disappeared.

Now on the way home everything seemed smaller than it had seemed when she first saw the train in June. Abby sat in her seat, staring ahead, thinking of home, of her father, and of what would be waiting at the farm and beyond the farm. She visioned the pine trees and the low country with the late summer grass on the fields as though on a grave. As a voice rasped affably she jerked forward in the seat.

"If it ain't Abby."

"Hello, Mr. Pratt."

"So you're going home, girl."

"I'm going home," she said.

Before her the shiny serge, the gold braid of the hat, and the gold teeth under it. Strange that he should be here at all. A million years had passed, a new age had arrived, a thousand trains had rushed up and down continents as far away as a darkest Africa that had seemed this summer, in the jungle of the mind, to begin to come alive in her, presaging a deeper night to come. Cars had gone through great deserts, up mountain ranges, and even in tunnels under water. Conductors had taken millions of tickets and scattered them away like leaves and gone to their graves, but here he was with the same toothy smile.

The Sea

THE seaman died on the day of the third albatross. A pale, cool day with a suggestion of the Cape rollers. A morning apparently no different from any other, and yet with his death the proportions of the vessel changed in the minds of those who inhabited it. When Dannie brought the news to the luncheon table Abby went as pale as the day. She felt almost as strange as she had felt the day her father died.

"Ticker stopped," Dannie muttered. "And de guy looked so strong down on de deck."

He had looked strong, his hair red and his skin sun-red, his shoulders big under his shirt. To watch his movements as he went about his work had made Abby feel strong, too. He'd been the one who waved when she came on deck mornings before beginning work on the book. He'd been the one, but she could not even name him. He'd been a person down there near the stanchion, breathing down there, watching the albatross. Only now he was dead.

"The captain will put him down in the sea," Dannie said.

The form would slide over the stern and the ship would circle the spot where they had put him down. All would be as it had been on the other vessel Smitty had spoken of so long ago. *And there are also celestial bodies and bodies terrestrial; but the glory of the celestial is one, and the glory of the terrestrial is another, for one star differeth from another star.* Each one of us dies a little each day, Abby thought, leaving the lounge behind her for the clean air of the deck.

"I'll bring you a coat," Dannie said. "Cold on deck today."

When he brought the garment she threw it over her shoulder and walked to the spot by the rail that had become her own. Last night the sailor had been with them on this sea the captain called a desert. Still breathing under Jupiter, Spica, Altair. Did the albatross fly at night? Did it keep watch over the ship? Where was God, anyway, and—Jim was right about it—why should she think He ought to have His eye on her?

This was the fourth night after the burial. Four days left to Cape Town and they might as well be four thousand. Topside, taking the watch that used to belong to Smitty before the captain demoted him, the fourth mate observed the sea as it swung upward toward the moon. Abby sat on deck near the radio shack with its blinking eyes and boards that flashed electric fire, wondering if tonight would bring another message from her brother

Henry. And would Henry send news of Jim? She thought of Jim with longing. The truth was that you died not one time but many. You buried one self along the way and then another. That was what she would, in the end, have to do for Jim. Bury the self-loving, self-demanding Abby she loved most of all.

It began to seem then that every part of the ship was encrusted with dirt from the shortened stack. On the deck were the usual blobs of soot, and above the deck chairs, trailing over the sea where the birds dip and swing, hung a plume of oily smoke. Abby wiped a black smudge from her cheek. She called out across the fringe of twilight to no one at all. And the profane words, moving out over the unlistening water, were a prayer.

"I have lived forever on this damned blue crazy ocean. My God, will I ever see Steeple Hill again?"

She watched a long roller licking at the tip of the roller in front of it. The sea *was* terrible. Better anything than those black-tipped waves. Better Jim in one of his rages when he slapped her after a party. *Whore—bitch—all those people hanging like crows in your past and you resenting my talking to a girl with an inviting face. You —in your day you've done some inviting!* She could feel the cut of his fingers on her cheek and the anger that was in the room like fog—no, like death.

You get buried so many times, she thought, watching the stars beginning to ride their courses over the cold sky. You get killed and buried, but that is not the end.

You get up out of the sea and begin the voyage again. You come alive, and you are with the others on the ship, even though part of you has been left to explode, or perhaps to rot in the shallows. You begin to breathe again, to feel need again, to feel desire, to think about going home. Then you lie back in your chair wondering suddenly—and shocked that the thought should come at all —whether Jim still wants you.

And what did the psychiatrist say to her when she had gone to him a long time after the crack-up was seemingly behind her? The Chinese one with his carved face and small brown hands. What did he say when she went to him to try to find out whether Jim had slapped her because she deserved it, or because she did not deserve it. A witch doctor of the psyche, that man Gordon Lin, weaving a spell around her, or maybe she had woven it around herself, watching his brown mask of a face.

"So you dreamed of being in some store?" The English was as soft as the silk of a mandarin's gown. "And you were caught there by a policeman?"

"As I remember it, that was the dream."

"And then?"

"Then my hands were full of sapphires—blue-white, flashing everywhere. Bright as stars. Or lilies. But in the moment of my holding them they turned to sand. And the policeman took me away."

"Why are people arrested, Mrs. Brandon?"

"For many reasons."

"Why?"

"For stealing."

"For stealing what?"

Abby was silent.

"What do you want worth stealing?" The question again. "Can love be stolen?"

"I've tried," she sobbed. "I've tried."

The brown hands fell to his knees.

"You have been stealing all your life. And the sapphires are still sand in your fingers."

"I hate you!"

He bent toward her.

"Your mother—trying to steal her back from the grave." And in that soft voice: "The Lisa of the camp. That *was* thievery."

"That's over—long over."

And the bland face above the white of the coat.

"Your father. What of him?"

"I took from him. At the last, I stole from him when he was dying!"

"And your husband, Mrs. Brandon?"

She had put her hands before her face, the sobs coming again.

But Dr. Lin had been right. She knew that now. He had been right all along the line. Wanting love, wanting it too much, reaching for it as if it were a sphere you could snare. Trying to steal a gone face, gone in air, gone in the sea, trying to find that face in Jim. Only he could not be that for her. Nobody could be that for anyone. Jim in Steeple Hill, and whose face was he watching? Suddenly cold, Abby burrowed into her blanket. On the deck, with the sky for a companion, you really got acquainted with the night.

She looked past the radiogram Sparks had brought her, looked toward the stern of the ship, thinking again of the flag-draped form. Sparks had said that after you buried them they'd explode when they got down deep enough. Jim once said that you could explode without going anywhere at all. Had he left her without going anywhere? There on the slope near the pool with the coed beside him—had he gone? If I wrote him, she wondered, if I wrote him and tried to tell him how it is—— But where was he now?

From the radio shack a British voice assaulted the air. *I can't give you anything but love, baby.* Abby pretended to make a decision. Then, suddenly, she knew the pretense for what it really was, and it was as if the knowing had been with her all the time. Staring at the blue-white water, she knew that she had never intended to leave Jim at Cape Town and perhaps not even at Zanzibar. And here was this radiogram, with the signature that of her brother Henry.

Her eyes turned again toward the yellow paper. And
the words burned into her again.

SEE THE FLOWER MARKET IN CAPE TOWN FOR ME.
AND WRITE JIM ABOUT HIS COED. HE'S GALLIVANTING.

Henry could tease when it amused him. And the shape
of the old-fashioned word that had once belonged to her
father might be part of the teasing. Or it might not be.
Was Jim on his way to class with the heat of the summer around him and with his thoughts a cloak against
heat, cold, sun, and sometimes against love? What had
he said once about the camp? *Women have so little in
the world that they should be allowed to have each
other.* He had told her to bury Green Leaf but the time
there was set into the record and was part of the larger
record.

If you called it a record, then he was right. *A tried
if trying existence is what we have together, Abby.* And
now she wanted it to be more than that. She wanted to
give him the understanding that he had given to her for
so long. Abby stood up, tearing the radiogram to pieces,
watching the little slips of paper fall like yellow butter-
flies into the sea. Was it too late?

A day comes, she told herself, or a night comes, when
you are demoted and deserve it. You'd gone too far down
the road to turn around, even though you think you've
just started. It is a death, not just of the body. The self
you loved too much and cherished too well has gone,

but nobody cares. And you must not blame anyone for not caring. Not the captain if you were a Smitty, and no —not Jim if you were you. She touched her damp forehead, leaving on her face a smudge of dirt picked up from the rail of the ship.

Abby was at her desk in the cabin after lunching with Telma Rosen. She read the words in her notebook and tried to think of the first port of call, close now, and of the plains beyond it.

> The green swamp and forest belt at Kitete conceals many buffalo and rhinoceros, and elephant and hippopotamus occasionally visit the place. Grant's gazelle, ostrich and impala will be seen on the way, as will giraffe, accompanied often by their young, who gaze with soft eyes at the car and sometimes allow it to pass within a few yards of them.

She flipped over pictures of the game at Gorongoza on the plains of Mozambique, a thousand miles south of Zanzibar. Lions with their yellow hides, ibis, vulture, and a hyena loping along with a bone in his jaws. And Eden-plain—and she was committed to go there before going home, or trying to go home—with zebra, impala, hartbeeste, kudu, and, most beautiful of all, the imperious sable antelope. But somehow the pictures were not important in the way they had once been.

She turned away from them, and went to the porthole to stare at a sea where many birds were now, the albatross with the wing almost touching the water yet never touching, and a brown line of gulls, great, fierce, riding close to the ship. Soon she would see the dolphin, the penguins, and the seals. And after that, on the lonely plains still far away, the lion, the leopard, and the gentle antelopes. *And will I smile His work to see? Did He who made the lamb make me?*

She turned and saw the letter slid under the door, and bent to pick it up. On the envelope in the neat, pin-fine writing, *Mrs. James Kirby Brandon, To Be Delivered Cabin Three, S. S. Dixie Belle, June 26, Courtesy Purser.* So the purser had slipped it there, as if it were a valentine, as if it were a square of bandage he had been keeping in that little lunch box of a first-aid kit of his, and had now taken out to stanch a cut or save a life.

> *Do not decide unless you are certain, for once it is done it cannot be undone. And come safely to harbor in Cape Town. Look at Table Mountain for me and tell me if it is what it seems to be in the picture books. When I read that there are peaks called the 12 Disciples, I always envision the Last Supper and wonder why they didn't name one Jesus. See the one called Lion's head—and take your time.*

With a small breath that was somehow a cry she placed Jim's letter on the desk and stood up tall, as if lightened at last of a too-heavy cargo. *See the one called Lion's head . . . and take your time.* At the porthole she watched the birds, and thought of the harbor not far away. *He maketh him to have dominion over the fish of the sea, the fowl of the air—and over myself?* Over myself?

At the bow of the ship Abby waited with Mrs. Rosen for the first sight of Table Mountain rising like a monster from the sea. The blade of the prow cut the water into snowdrops. No image of a figurehead left. But the way that blade edge cut a path through the water, moving always toward harbor, brought courage. And the remembrance of Jim's words was like sunlight.

Ahead, the harbor with seals and penguins, a mountain with a lion's head—*look at Table Mountain for me.* A wharf where the ship would dock for one night only before moving forward again out of the Atlantic and into another sea. Cape Town, and for some people it was the home Charleston had been for her that last day —so long in the past—when she had left it behind and leaned over the rail to see the color of the deep. Abby looked up. Before her, misty like the mountain ranges of home, a faded blue over the cold sea, lay the land! The land!

So Africa was outside of her, after all.

It was like a dream with the mountain more blue than before but still not made of dirt and rock. This dream, very real while it lasted, was part of a larger one that she did not yet understand. She knew only that they seemed to be alive, and that they swam on the sea for a while and then, like the gone sailor in his weighted canvas, dissolved into the deep. For all must go down, and through the going come to the deeper face of the dreaming that would always be hid from those whose dive was still to come. And God, like the captain on this voyage from the cape of fear to the cape of good hope, would He always be upstairs?

"Come back to the deck with me." Dannie spoke from beside her.

As they left the bow, the harbor was closer with each forward dip of the *Belle* through the sea. Over the prow the water that was like snowdrops broke and fell; from the stern appeared a light blue wake, and almost 7,000 miles behind it lay the home in Steeple Hill she hoped to find again when the journey was over. Everywhere the birds flying over the sea that with land so close was no longer terrible.

Abby stood on the cabin deck watching the sailors as they worked on the deck below. Standing then in the shade of the lifeboat above her, with its canvas-covered engine that might not last through the first rough sea, she watched the water where a seal swam by. Behind the sea was the mountain, brown in the sun, and on its slopes the protea she would see in the flower market in the town. Africa was a giant, and strange. Quiet, she watched the harbor. Ahead lay the Indian Ocean. Beyond that the Pacific. And then that point beyond which any direction was home.